INVADERS
FROM THE GREAT GOO GALAXY

Librarian Reviewer
Laurie K. Holland
Media Specialist (National Board Certified), Edina, MN
MA in Elementary Education, Minnesota State University, Mankato

Reading Consultant
Mark DeYoung
Classroom Teacher, Edina Public Schools, MN
BA in Elementary Education, Central College
MS in Curriculum & Instruction, University of MN

Graphic Sparks are published by Stone Arch Books
151 Good Counsel Drive, P.O. Box 669
Mankato, Minnesota 56002
www.stonearchbooks.com

Library of Congress Cataloging-in-Publication Data
Hoena, B. A.
Eek and Ack, Invaders from the Great Goo Galaxy / by Blake A Hoena; illustrated by Steve Harpster.
p. cm. — (Graphic Sparks. Eek and Ack)
ISBN-13: 978-1-59889-052-5 (library binding)
ISBN-10: 1-59889-052-2 (library binding)
ISBN-13: 978-1-59889-225-3 (paperback)
ISBN-10: 1-59889-225-8 (paperback)
1. Graphic novels. I. Harpster, Steve. II. Title. III. Series.
PN6727.H57I58 2007
741.5'973—dc22 2006007697

Summary: Eek and Ack, two alien brothers from another galaxy, are egged on by their older sister, Bleck, to conquer Earth. When they arrive in a spaceship that looks like a washing machine, they get into some sudsy trouble.

Art Director: Heather Kindseth
Cover Graphic Designer: Heather Kindseth
Interior Graphic Designer: Keegan Gilbert

1 2 3 4 5 6 11 10 09 08 07 06

Printed in the United States of America

EEK & ACK

INVADERS FROM THE GREAT GOO GALAXY

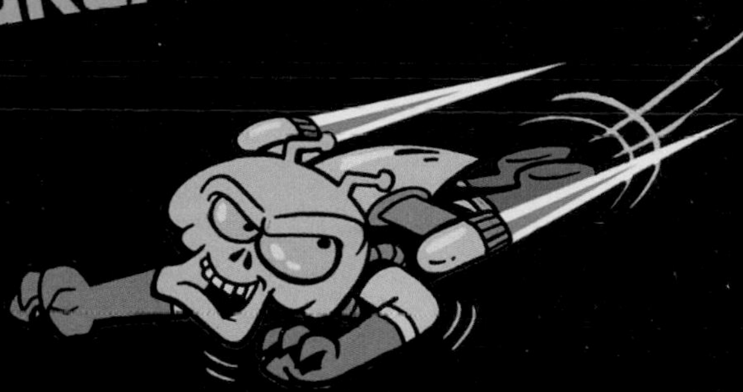

BY BLAKE A. HOENA

ILLUSTRATED BY STEVE HARPSTER

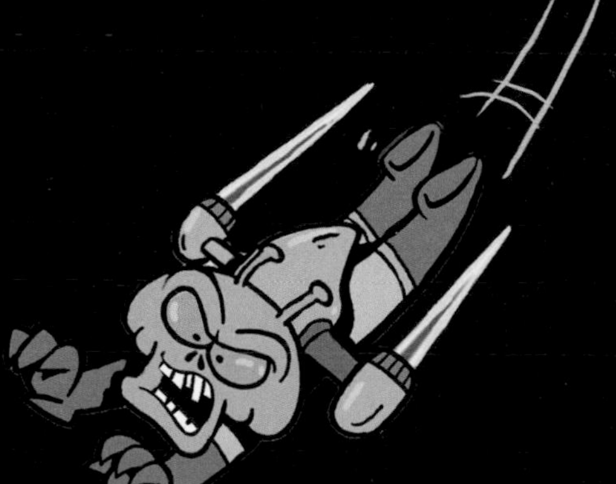

CAST OF CHARACTERS

Bleck - Eek and Ack's older sister

Eek - space alien kid

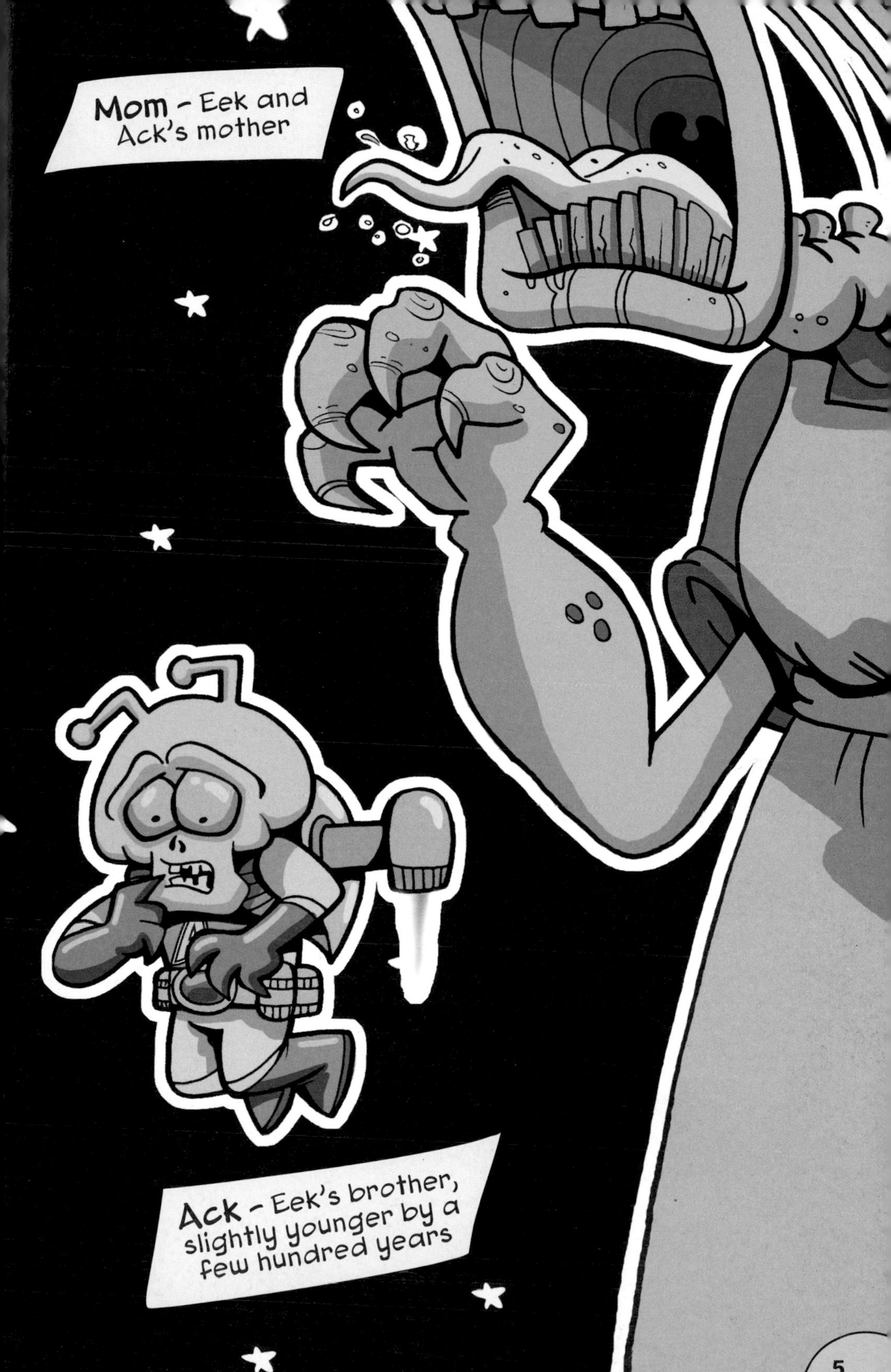
Mom - Eek and Ack's mother
Ack - Eek's brother, slightly younger by a few hundred years

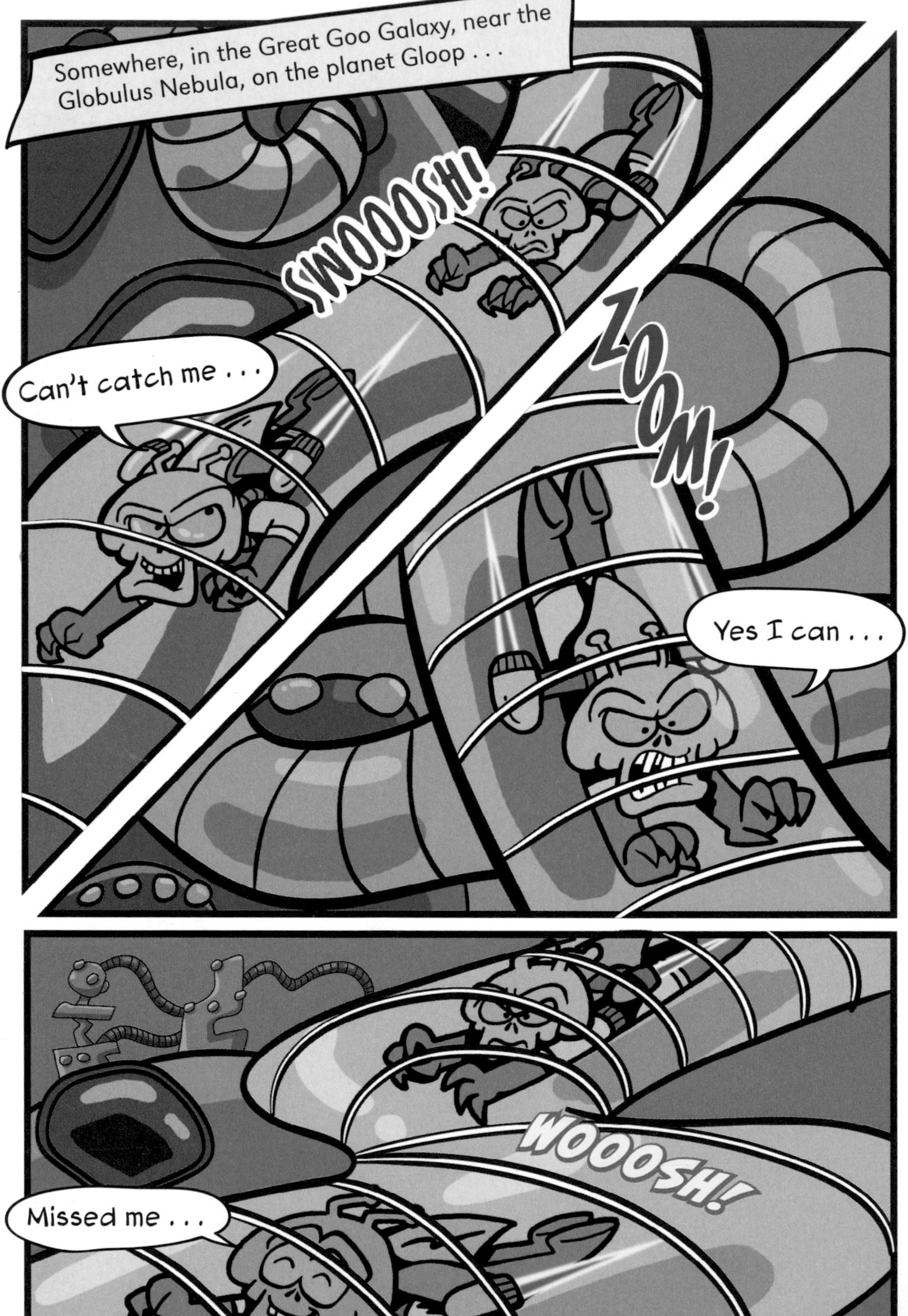
Somewhere, in the Great Goo Galaxy, near the Globulus Nebula, on the planet Gloop . . .
SWOOOSH!
Can't catch me . . .
ZOOM!
Yes I can . . .
WOOOSH!
Missed me . . .

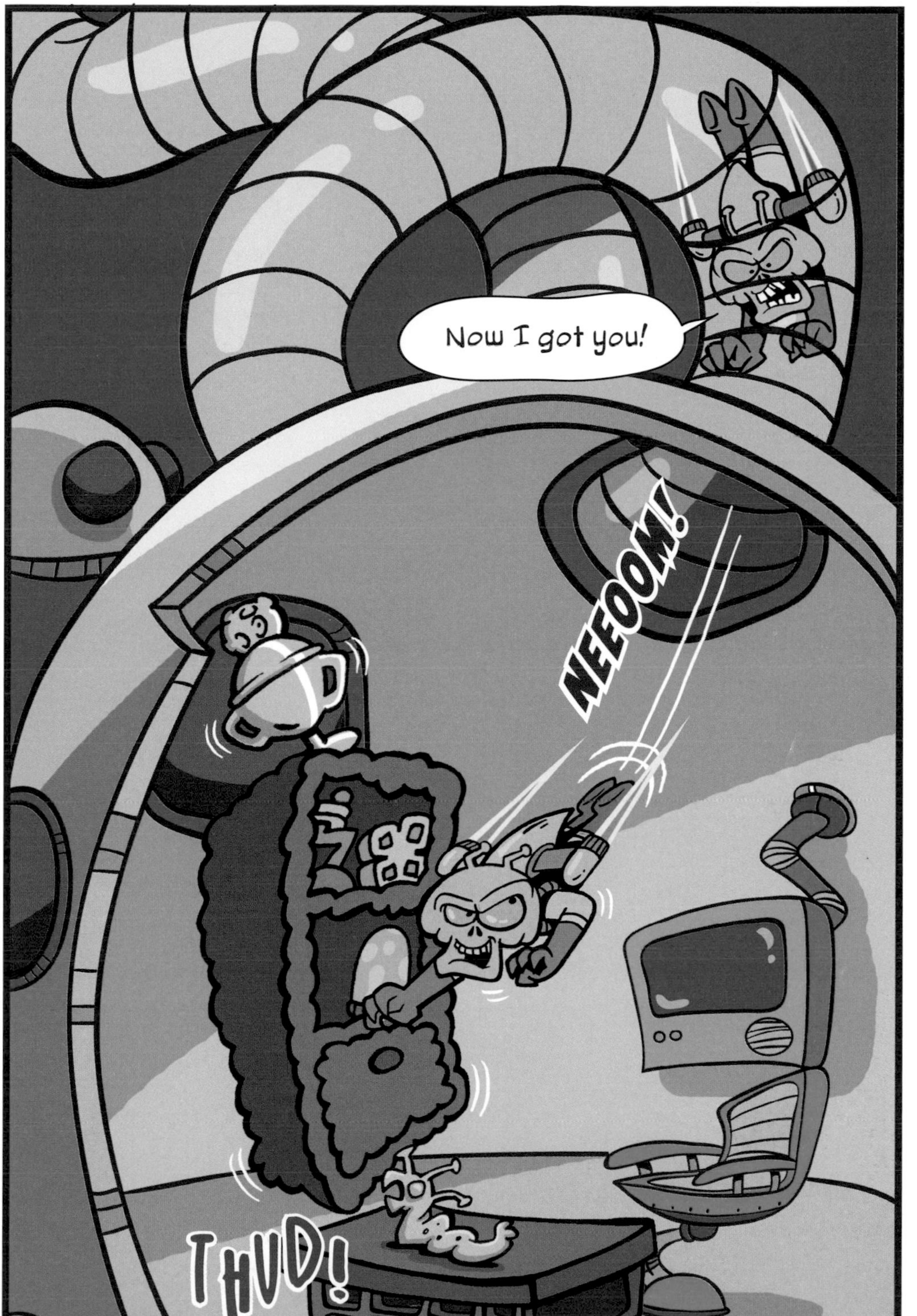
Now I got you!
NEEOOM!
THUD!

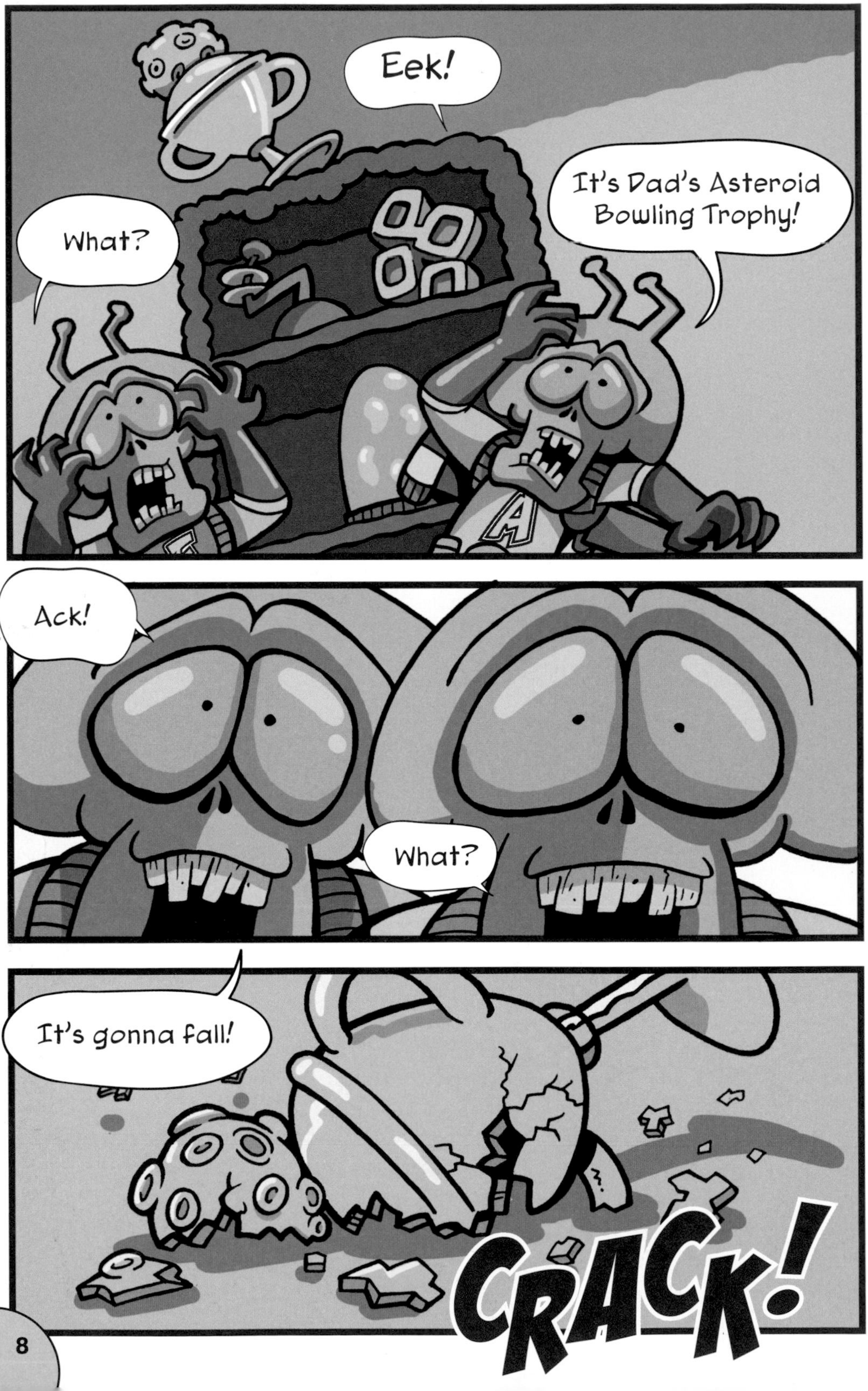
Eek!
What?
It's Dad's Asteroid Bowling Trophy!
Ack!
What?
It's gonna fall!
CRACK!

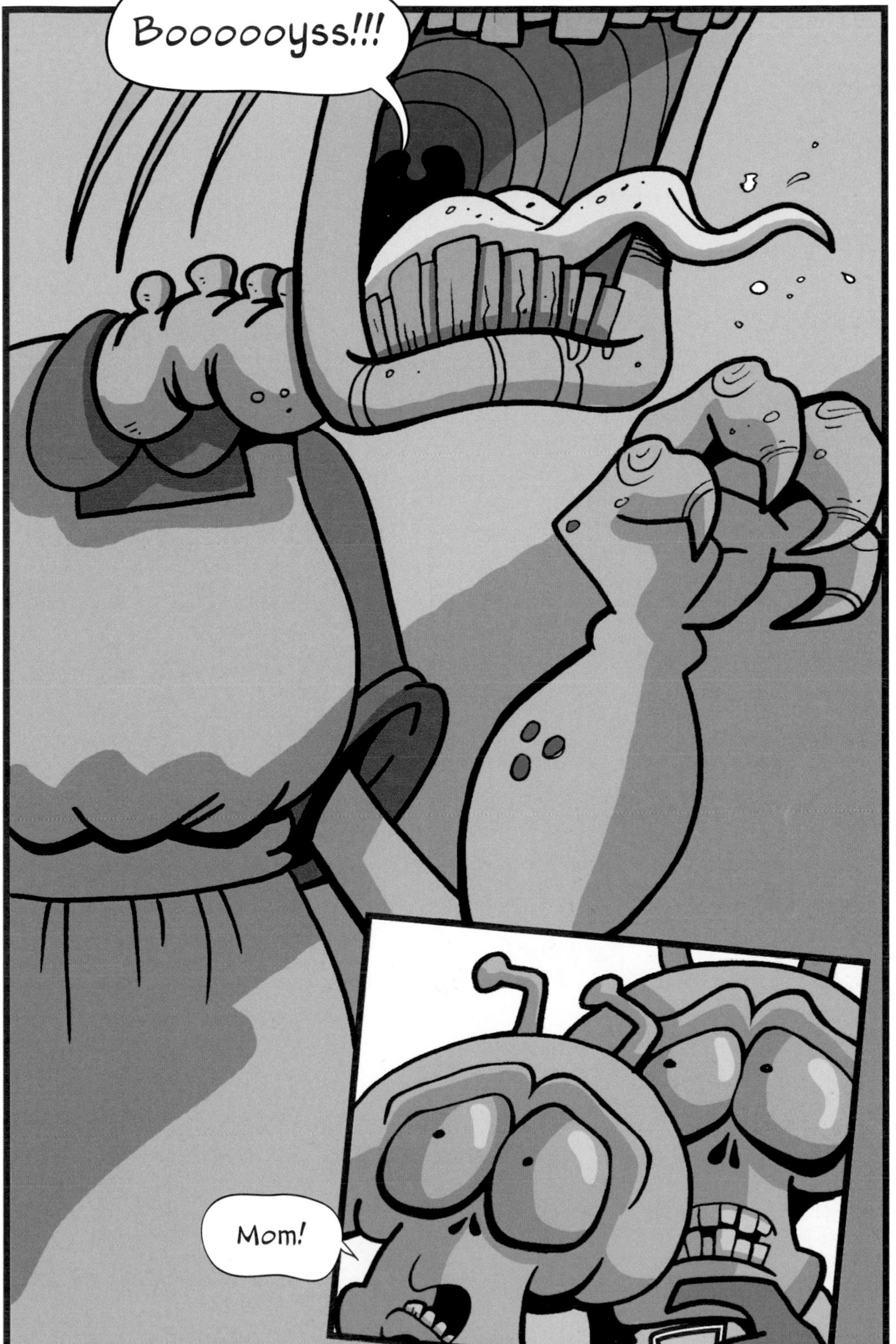
Booooooyss!!!
Mom!

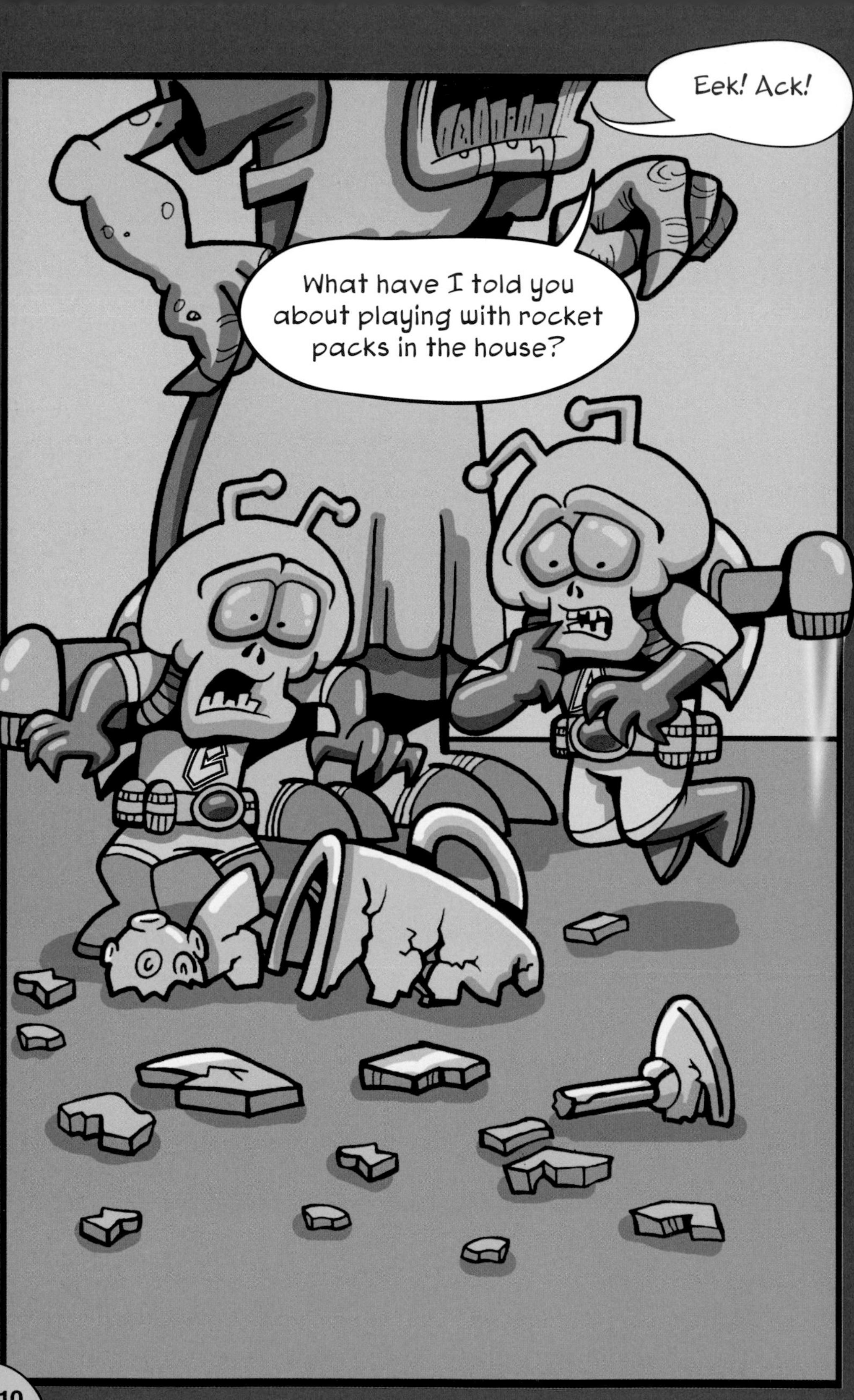
Eek! Ack!
What have I told you about playing with rocket packs in the house?

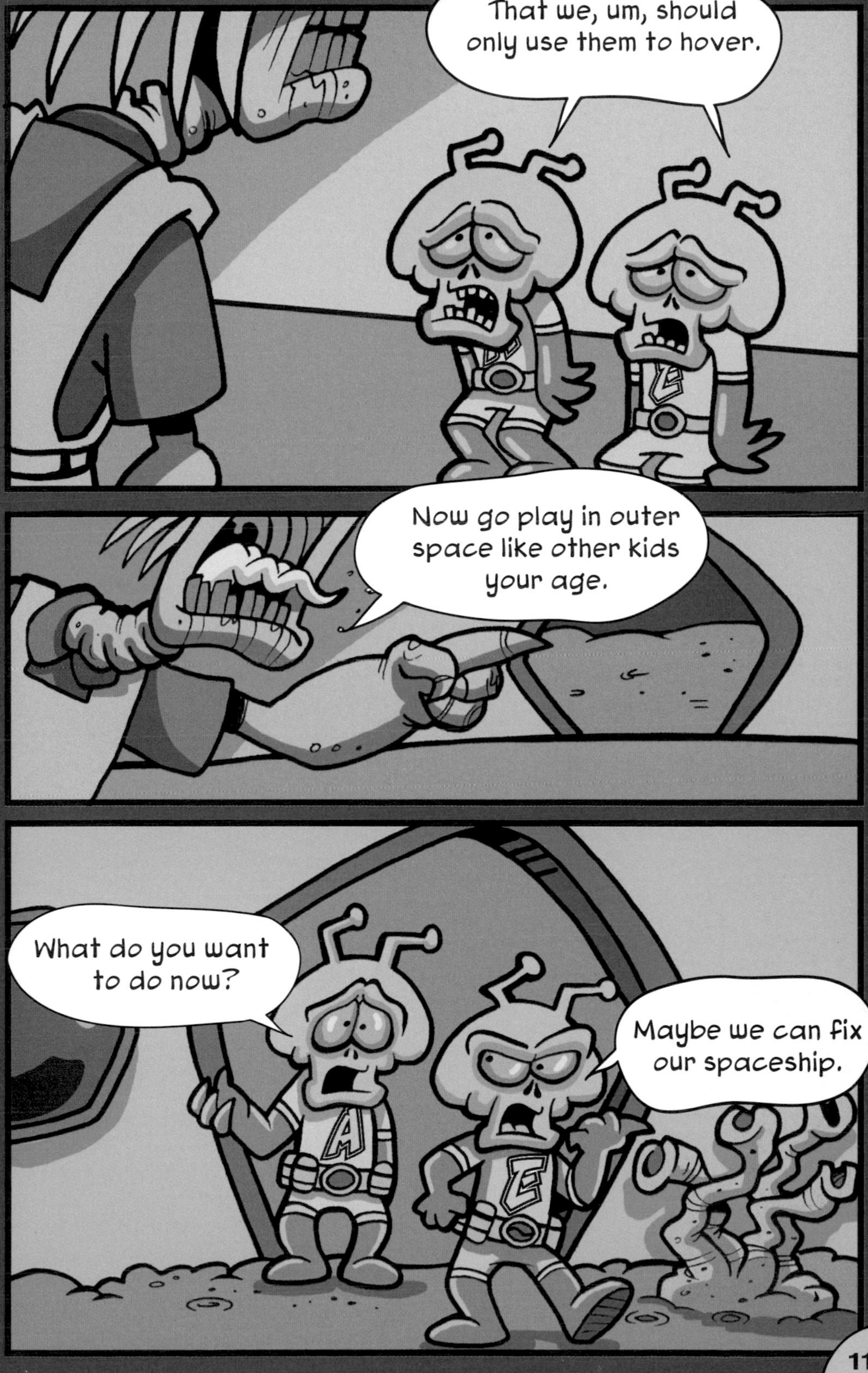
That we, um, should only use them to hover.
Now go play in outer space like other kids your age.
What do you want to do now?
Maybe we can fix our spaceship.

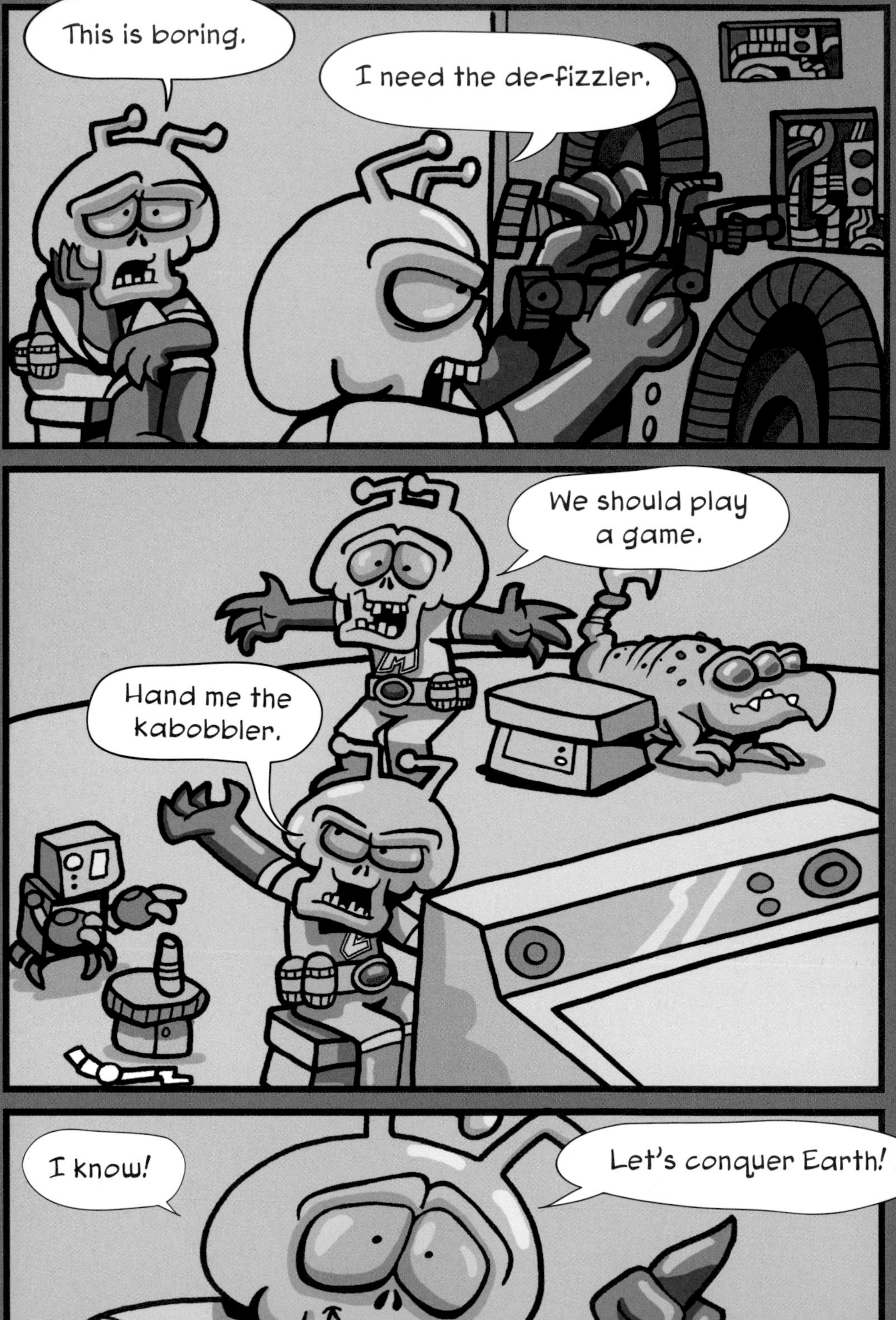
This is boring.
I need the de-fizzler.
We should play a game.
Hand me the kabobbler.
I know!
Let's conquer Earth!

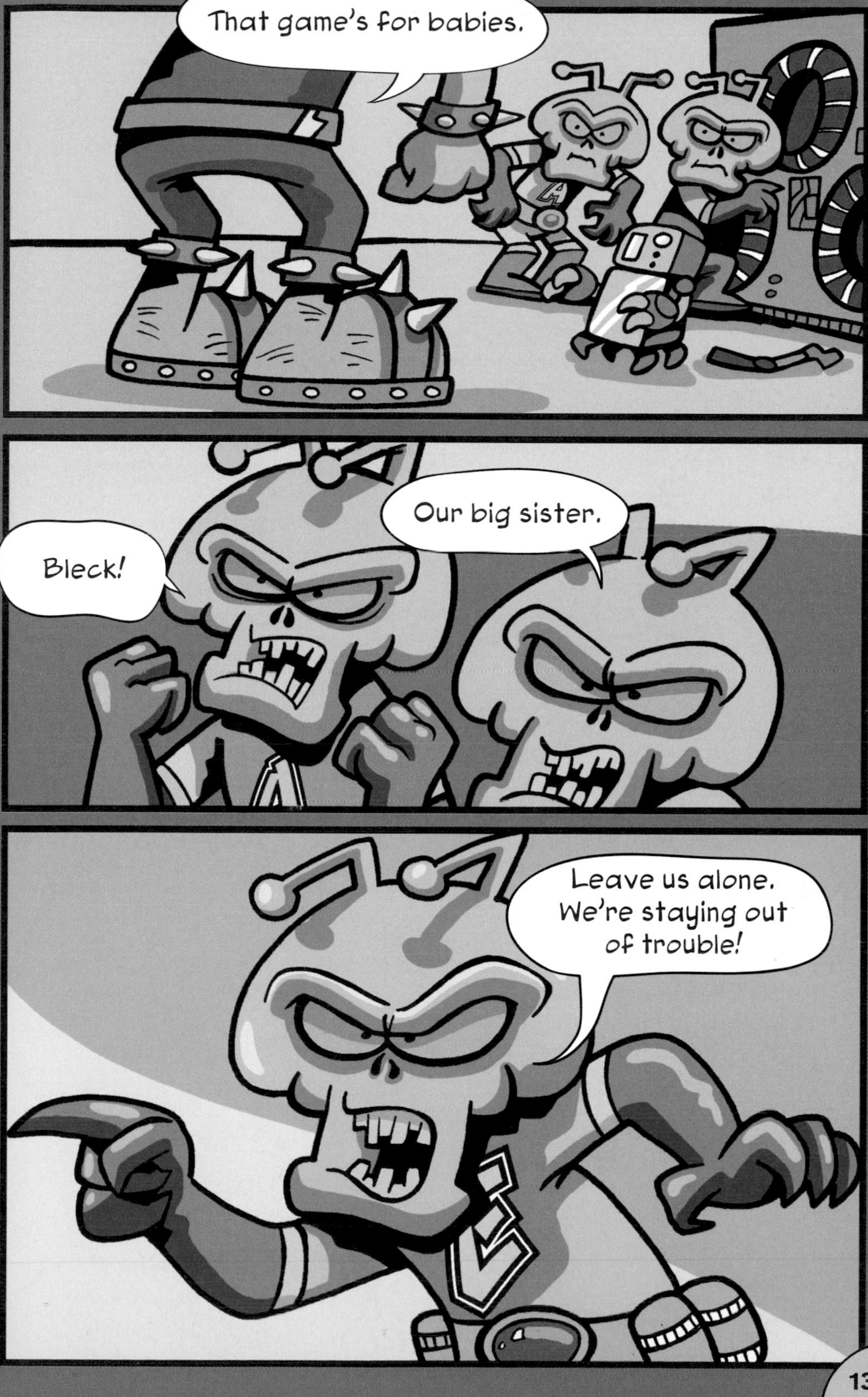
That game's for babies.
Bleck!
Our big sister.
Leave us alone. We're staying out of trouble!

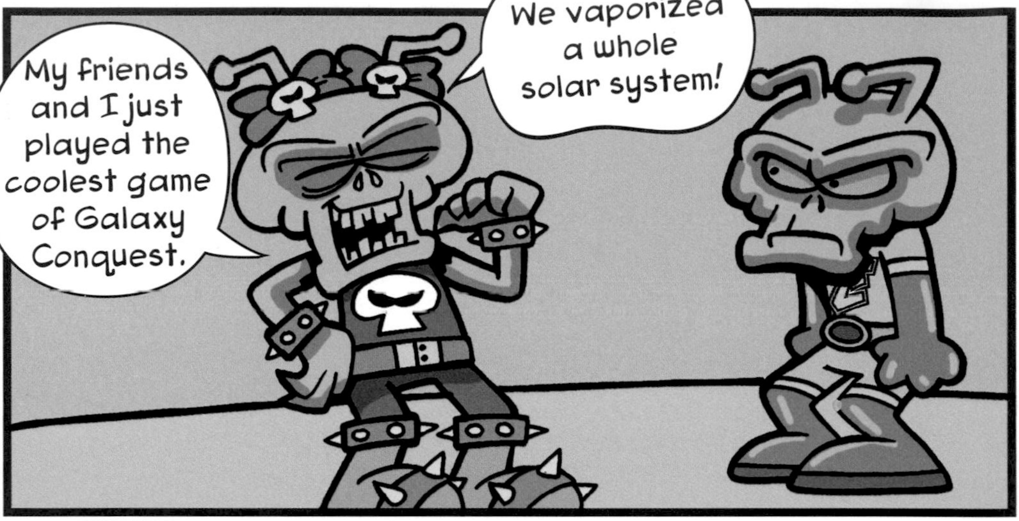
My friends and I just played the coolest game of Galaxy Conquest.
We vaporized a whole solar system!

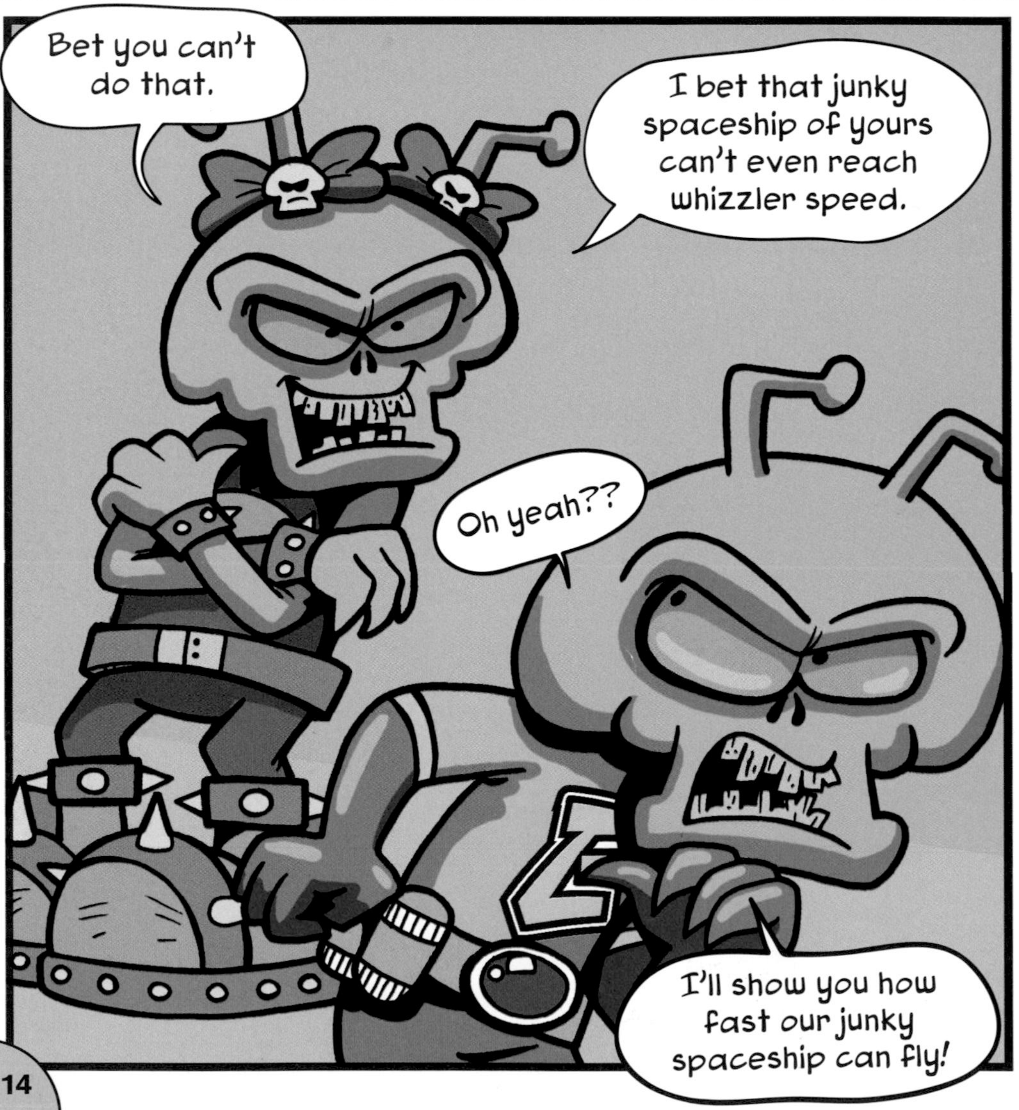
Bet you can't do that.
I bet that junky spaceship of yours can't even reach whizzler speed.
Oh yeah??
I'll show you how fast our junky spaceship can fly!

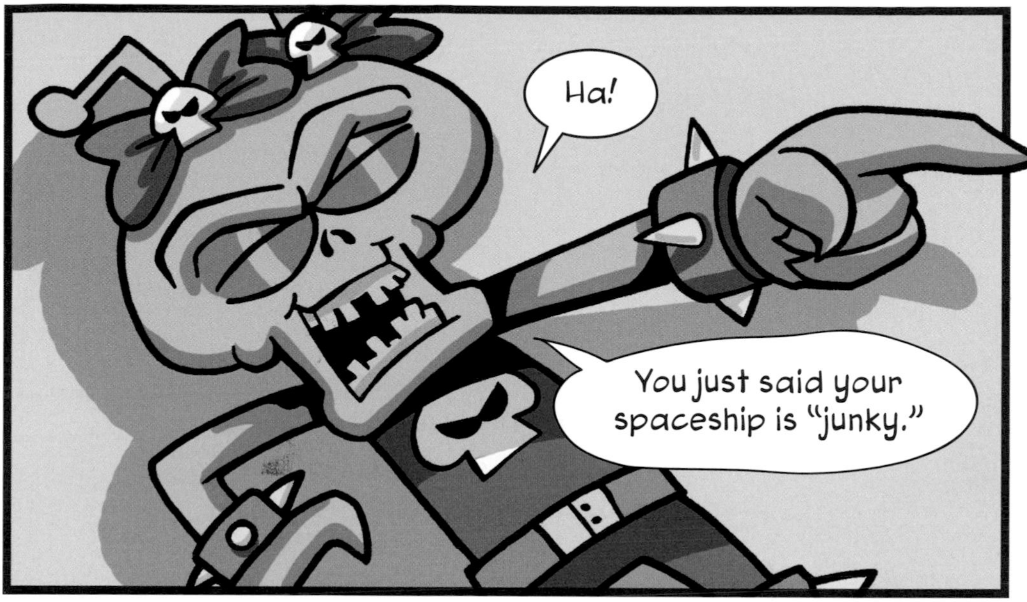
Ha!
You just said your spaceship is "junky."

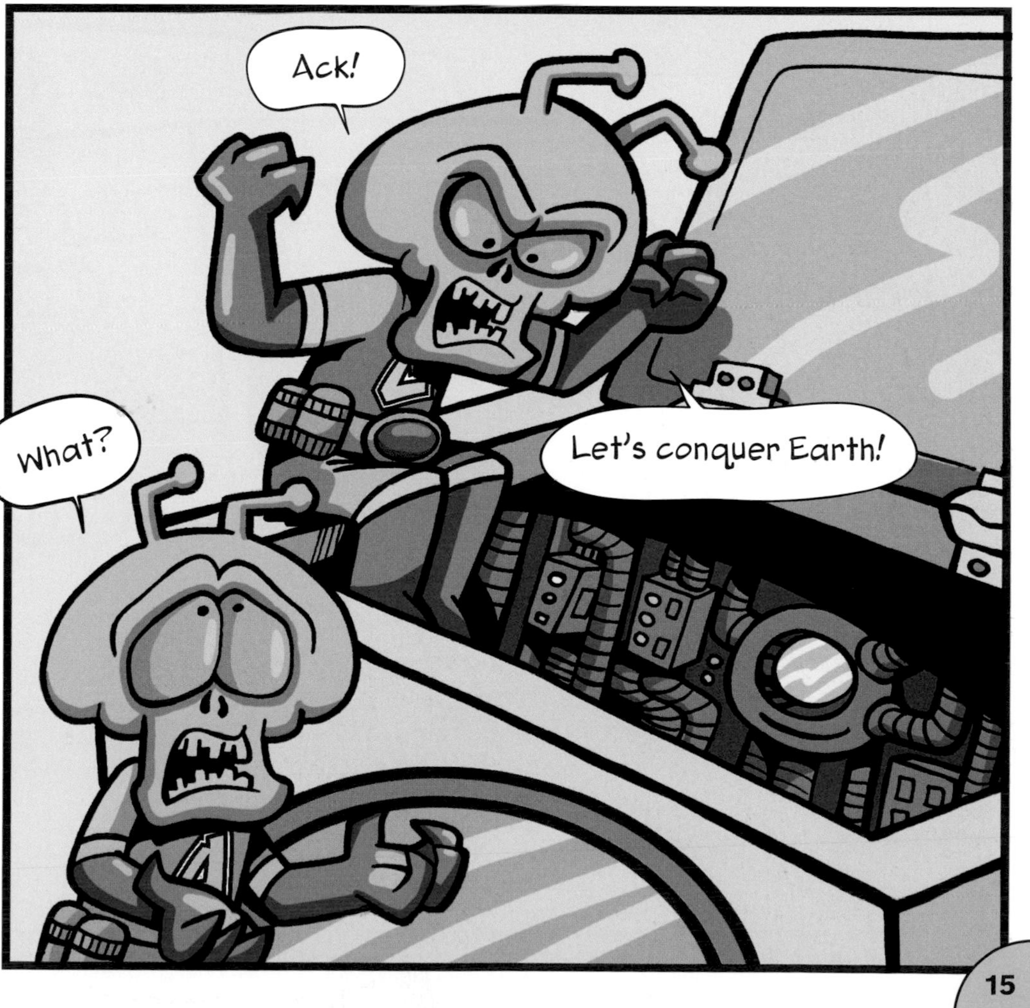
Ack!
Let's conquer Earth!
What?

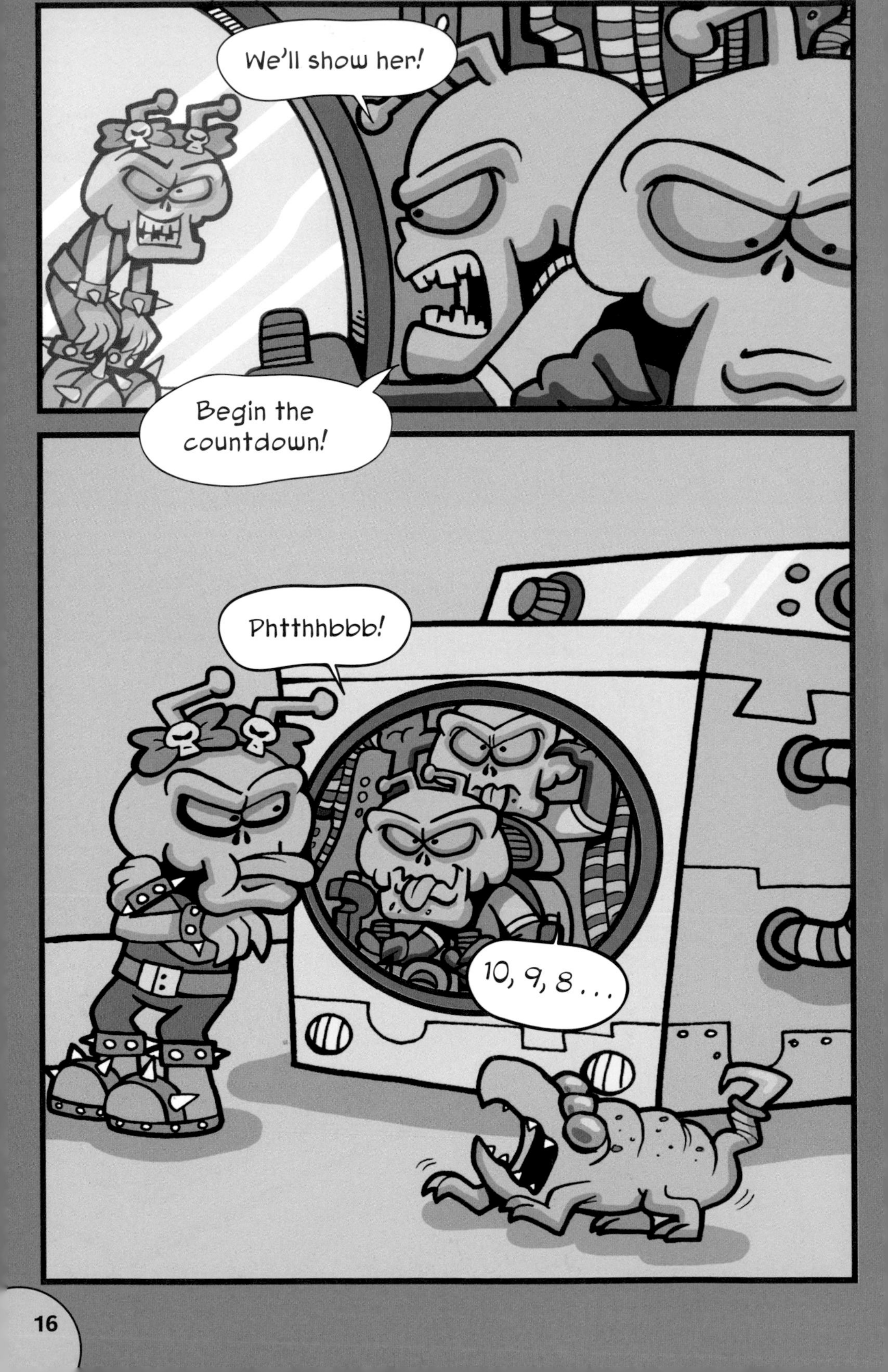
We'll show her!
Begin the countdown!
Phtthhbbb!
10, 9, 8 . . .

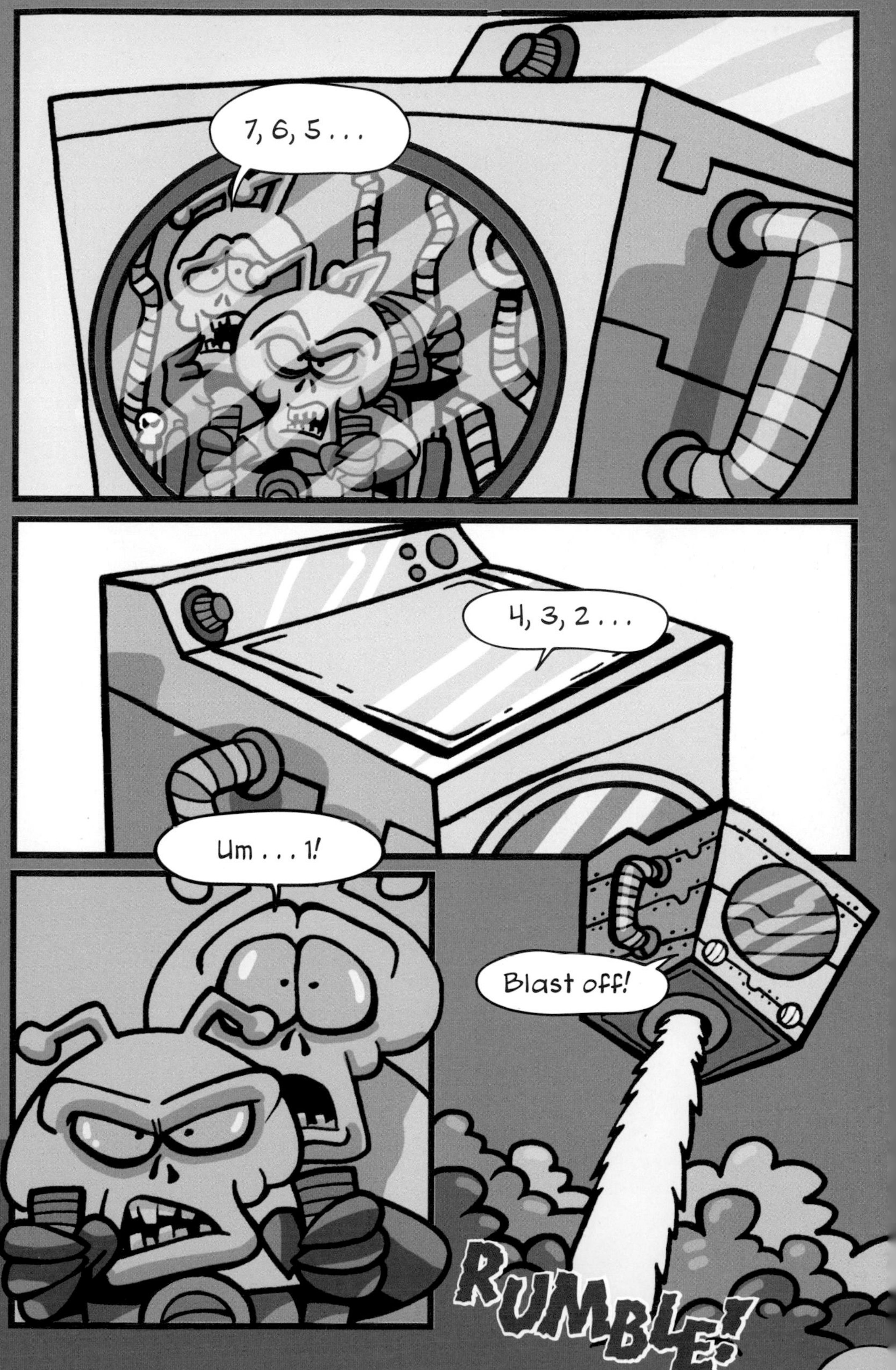
7, 6, 5 . . .
4, 3, 2 . . .
Um . . . 1!
Blast off!
RUMBLE!

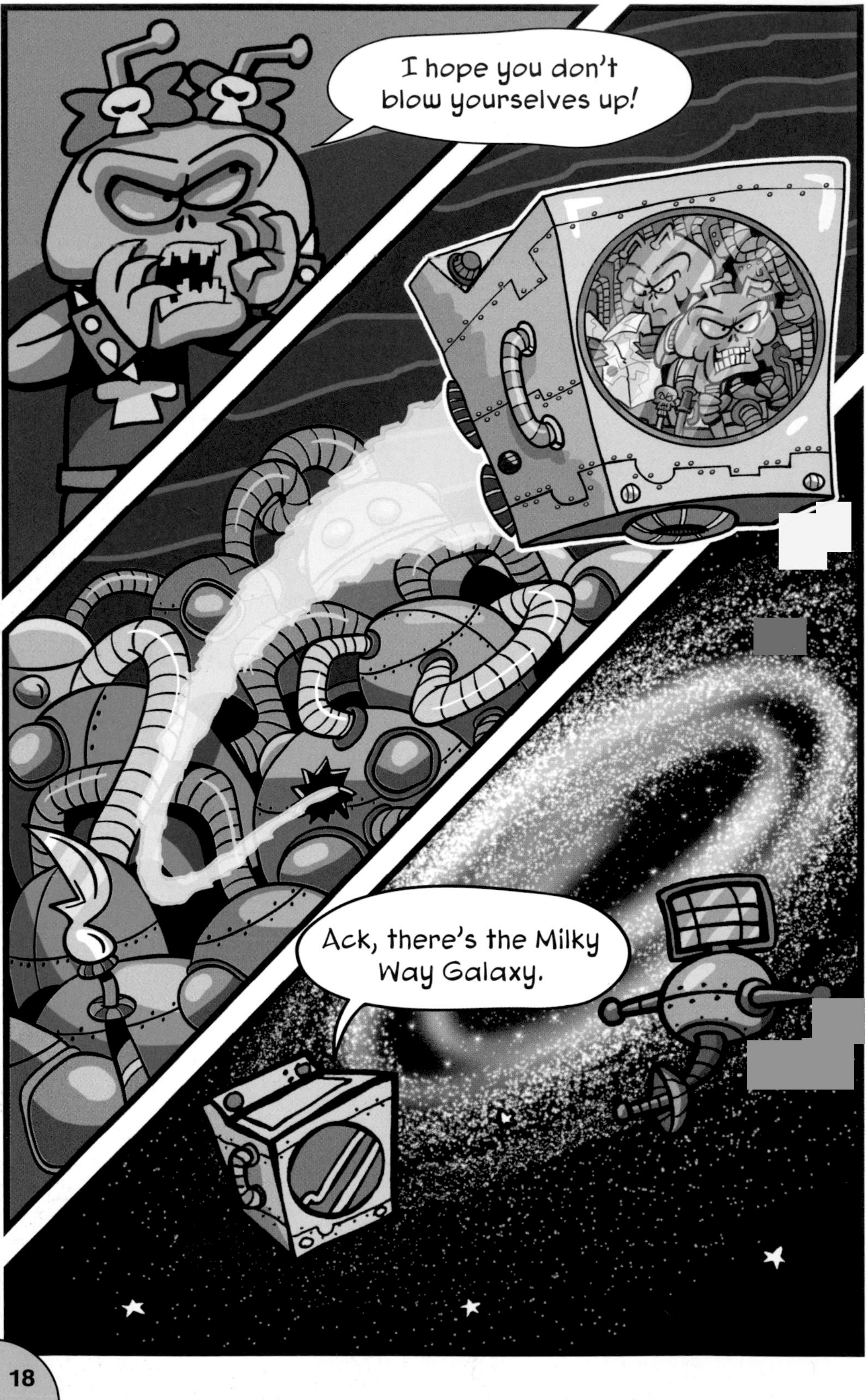
I hope you don't blow yourselves up!
Ack, there's the Milky Way Galaxy.

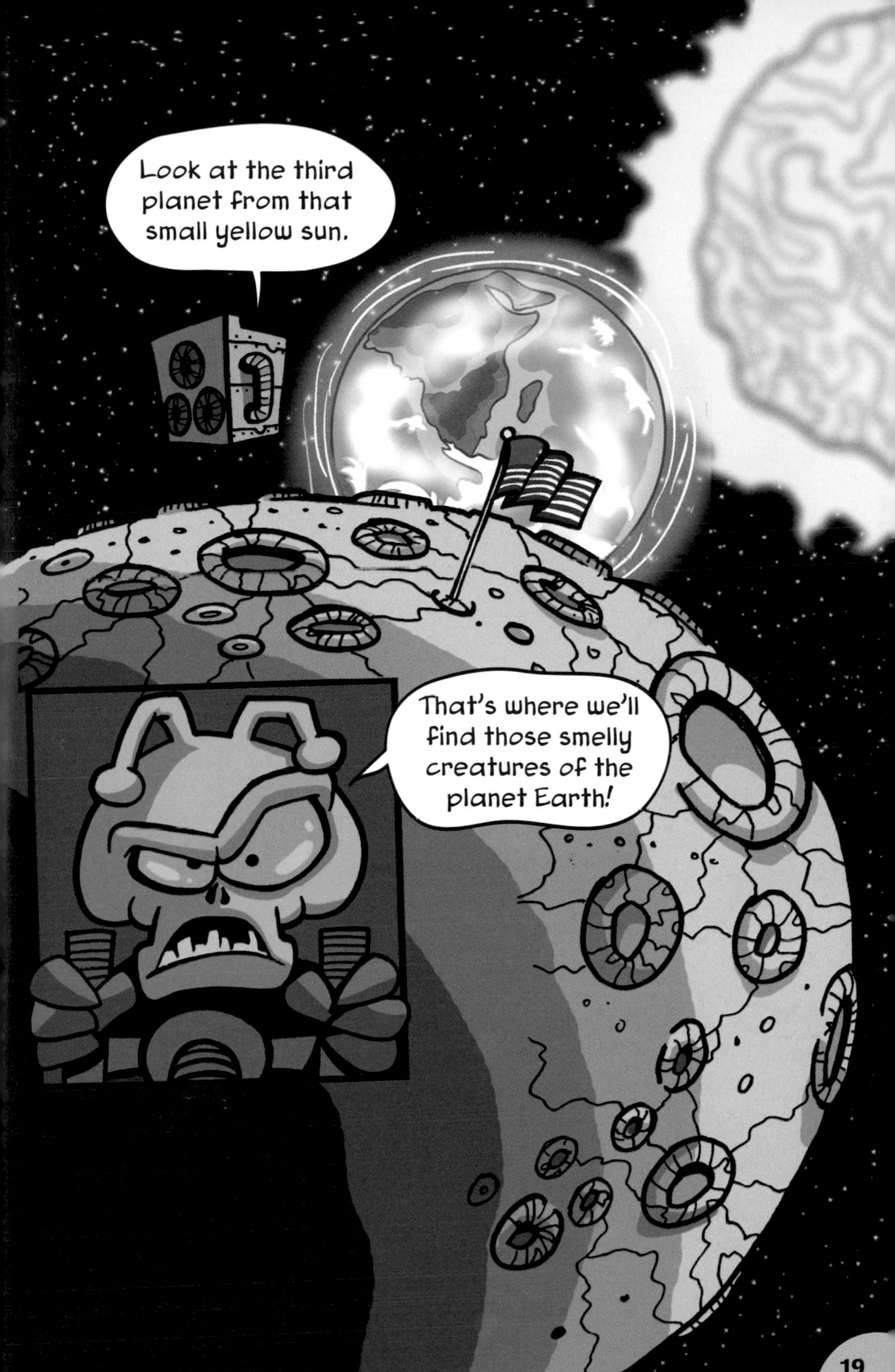
Look at the third planet from that small yellow sun.
That's where we'll find those smelly creatures of the planet Earth!

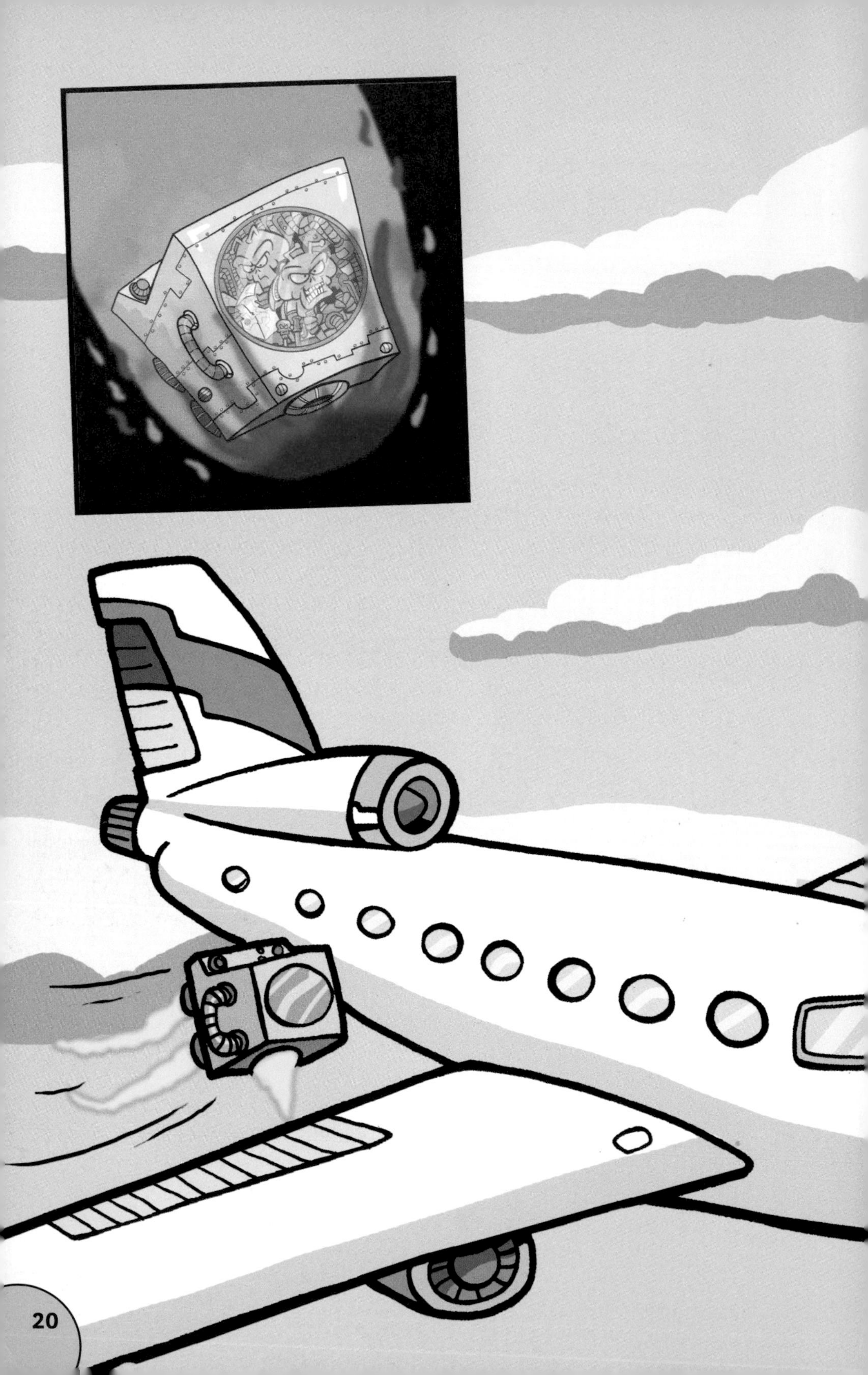

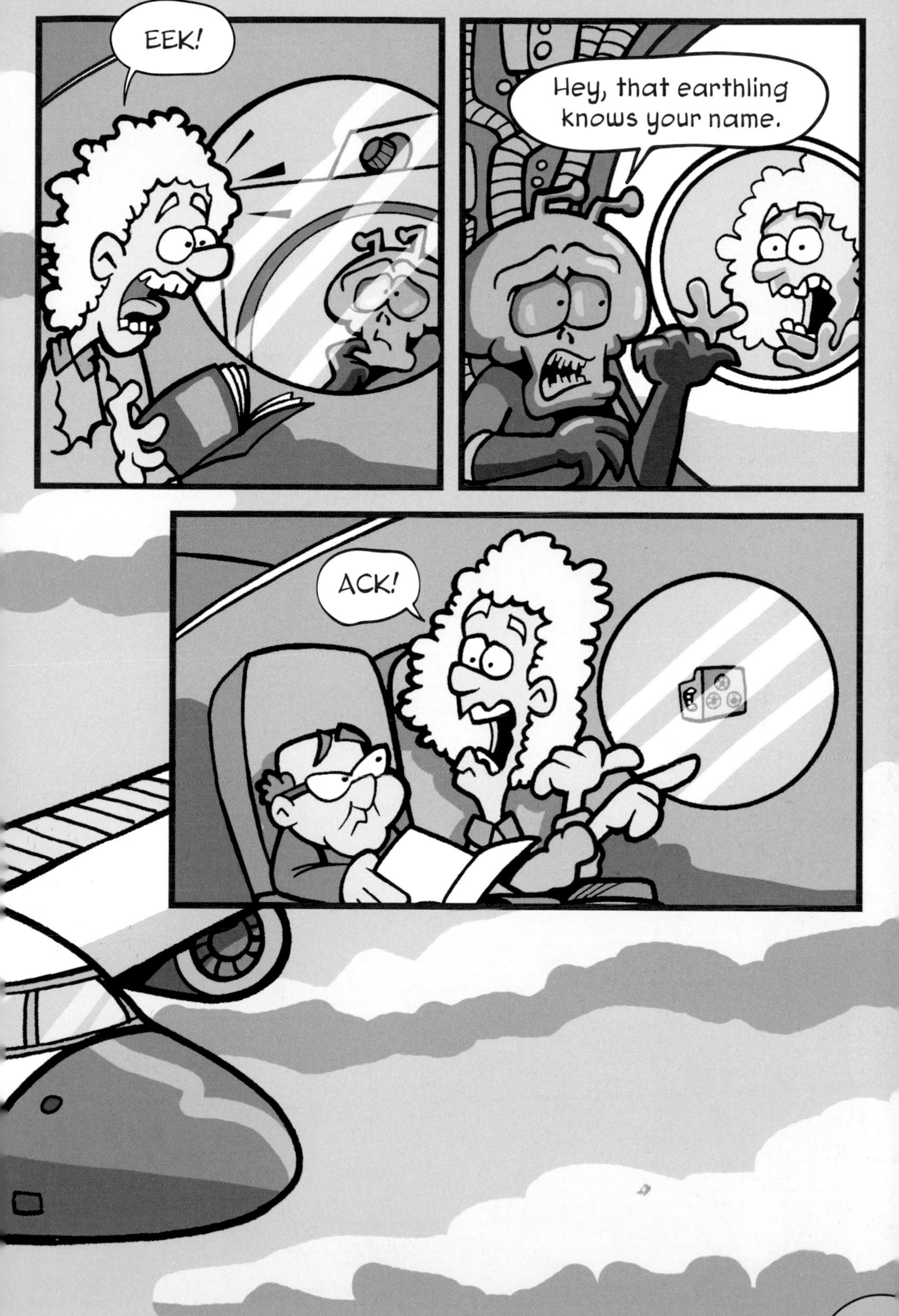
EEK!
Hey, that earthling knows your name.
ACK!

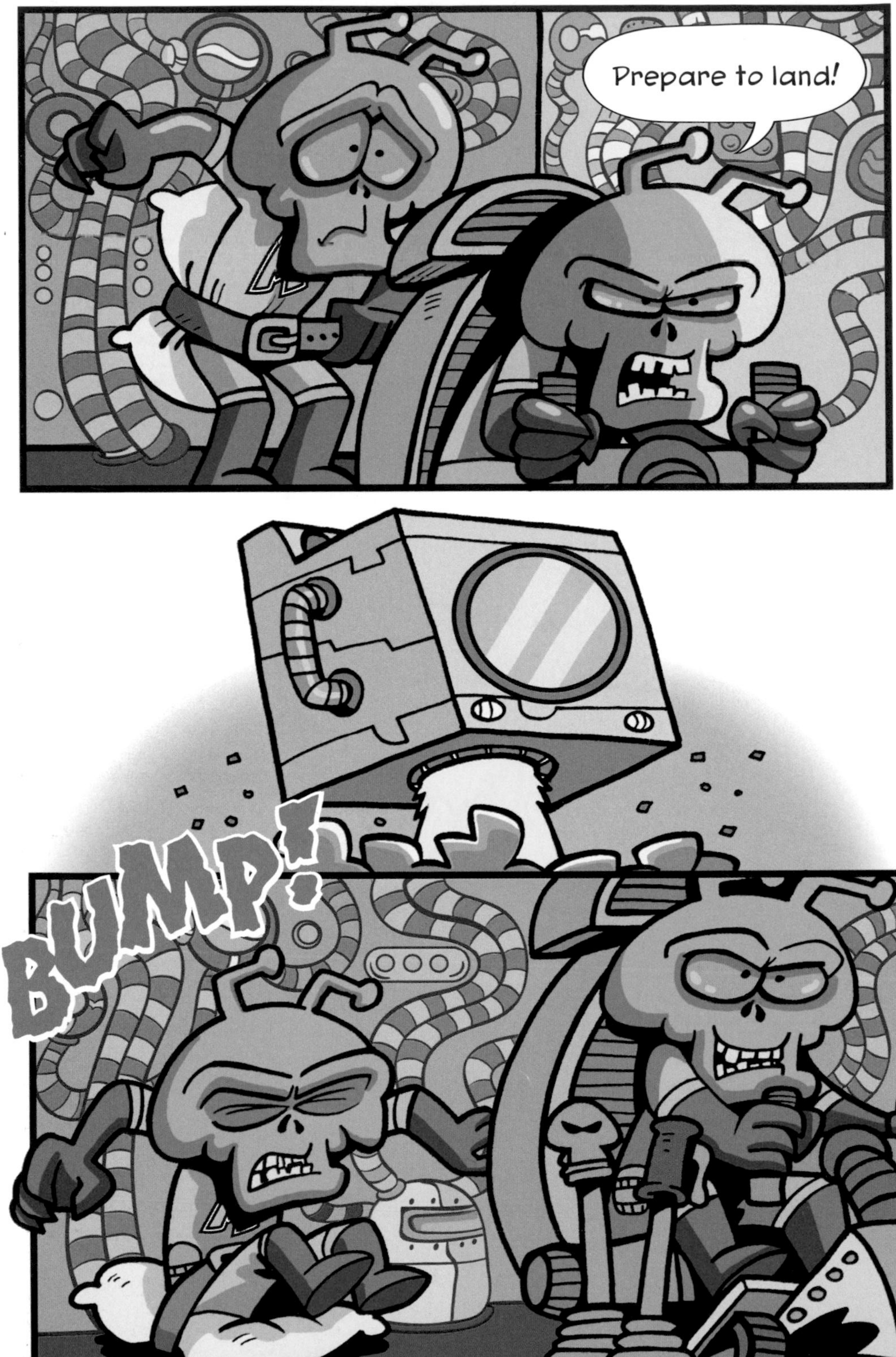
Prepare to land!
BUMP!

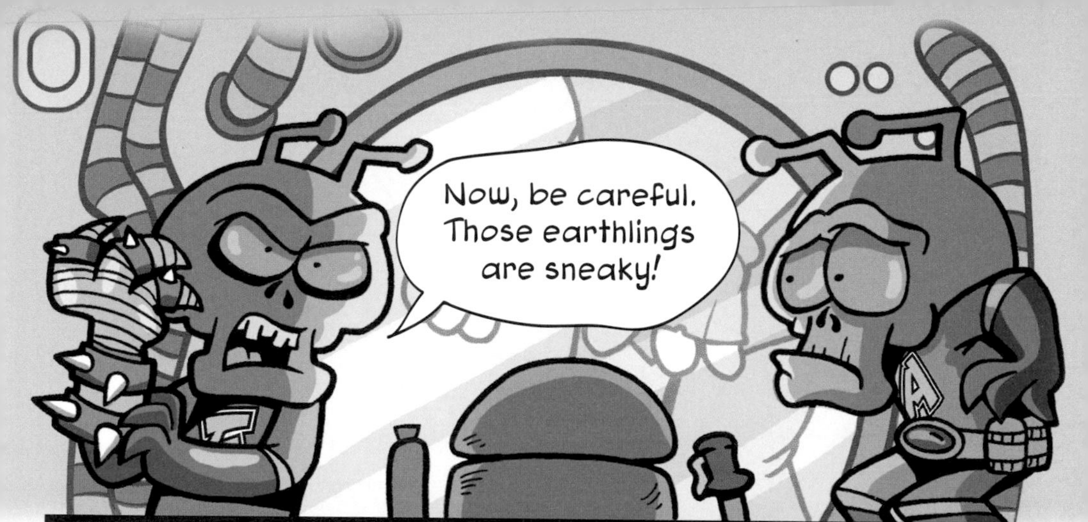
Now, be careful. Those earthlings are sneaky!

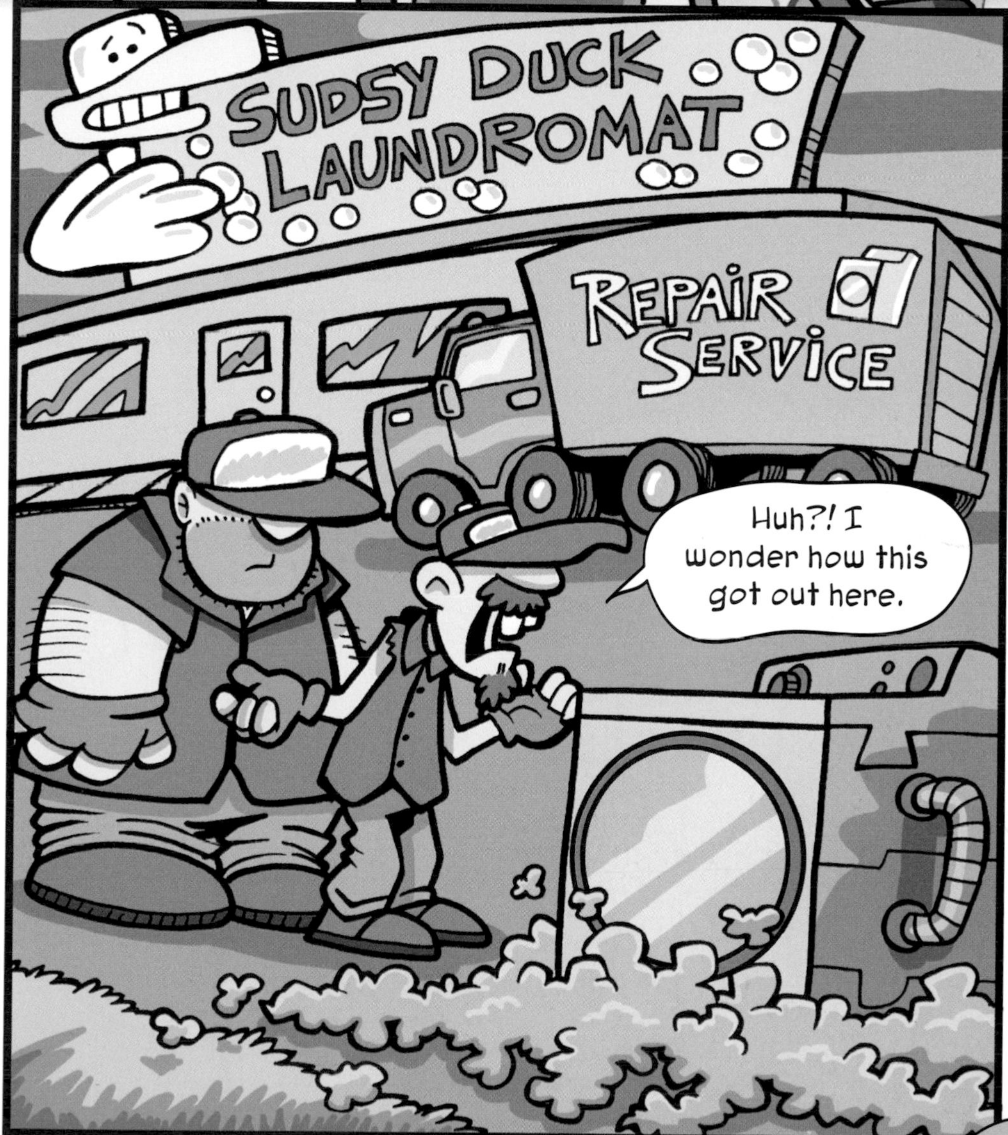
SUDSY DUCK LAUNDROMAT
REPAIR SERVICE
Huh?! I wonder how this got out here.

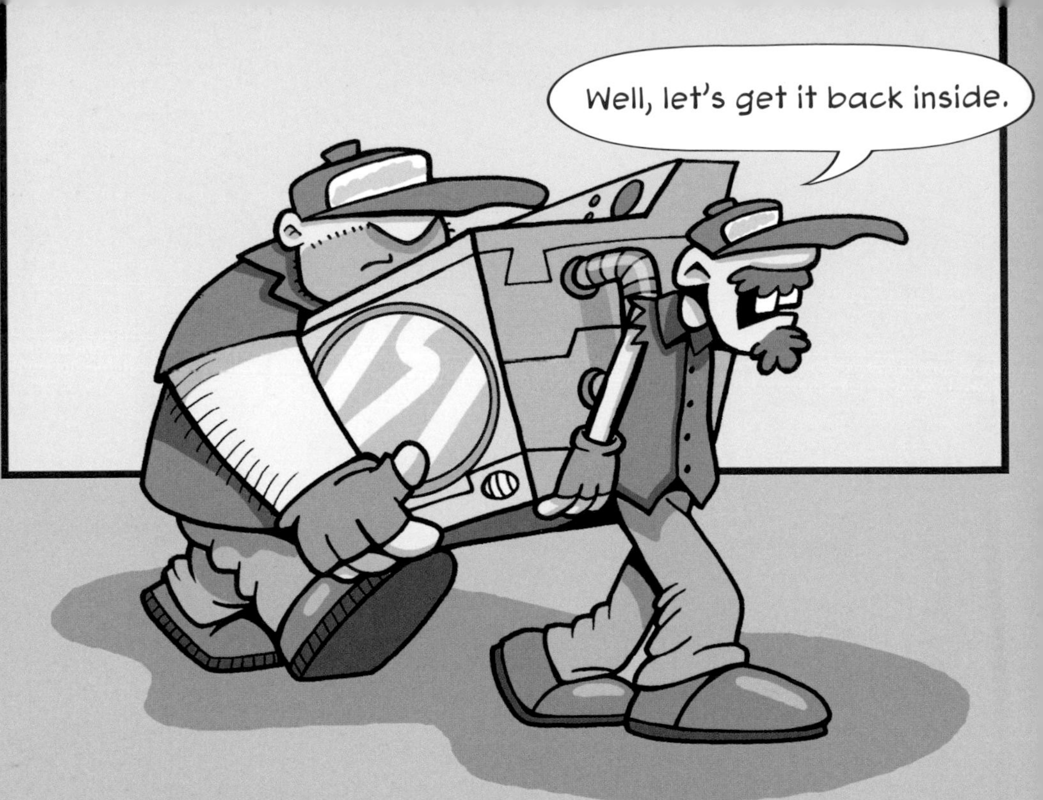
Well, let's get it back inside.

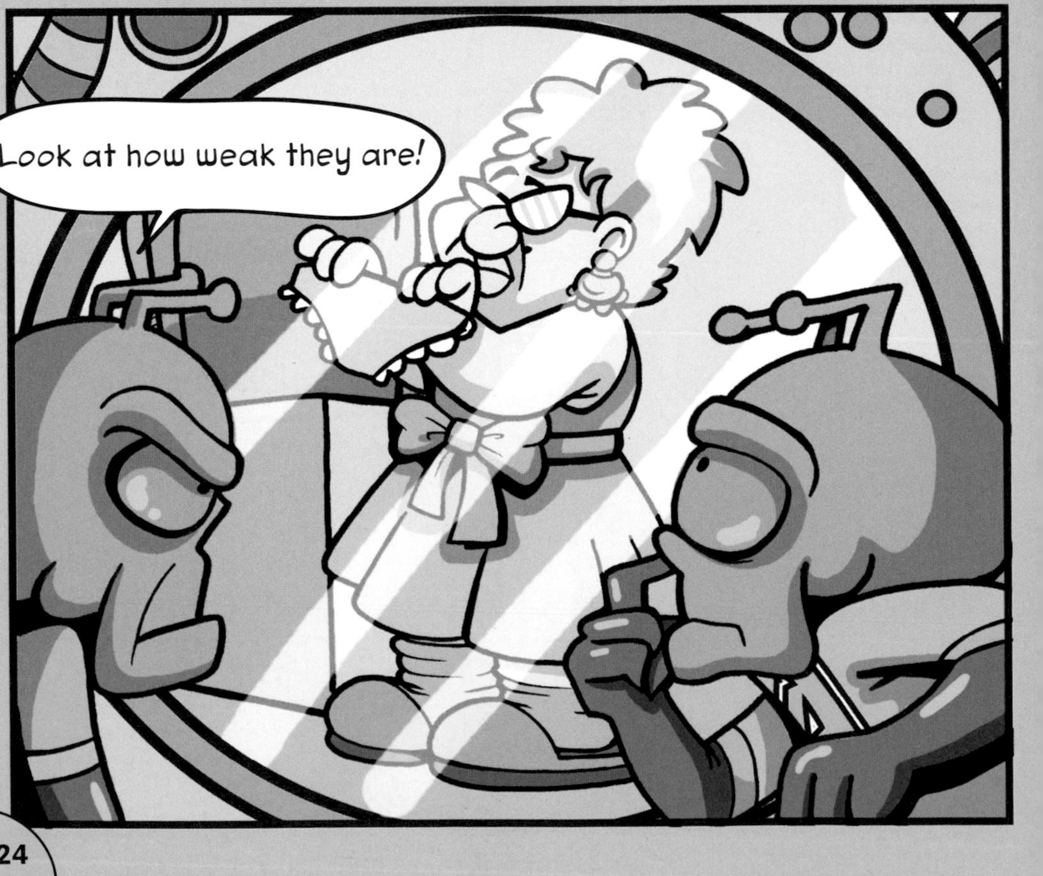
Look at how weak they are!

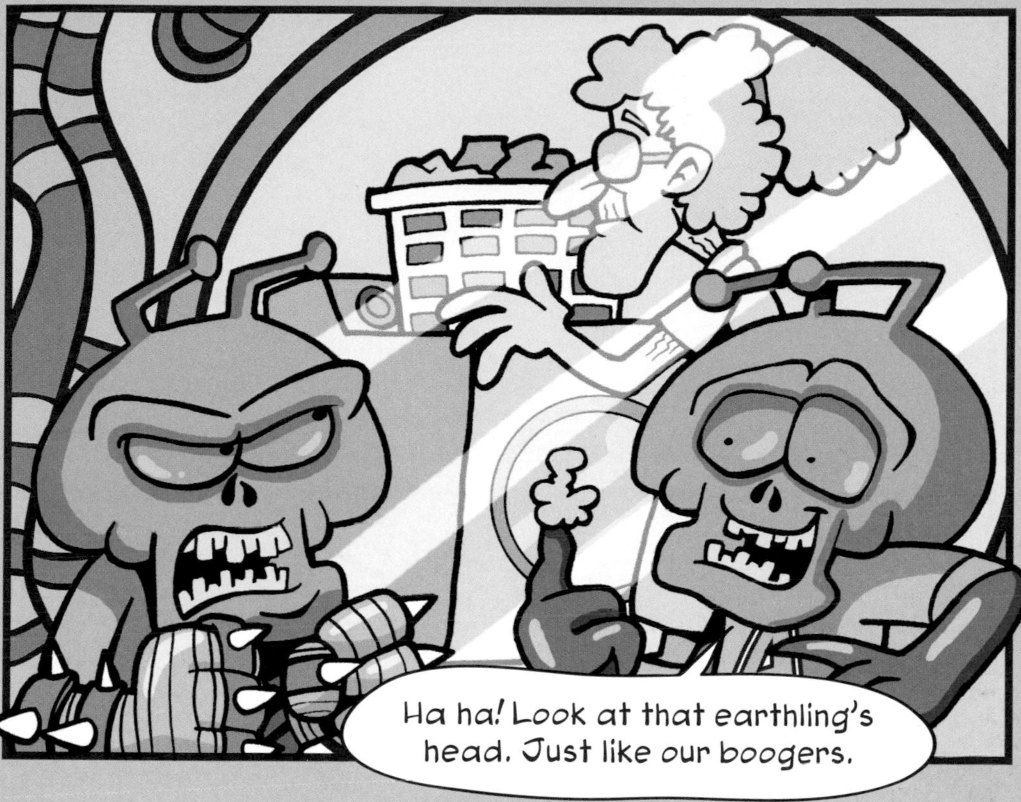
Ha ha! Look at that earthling's head. Just like our boogers.

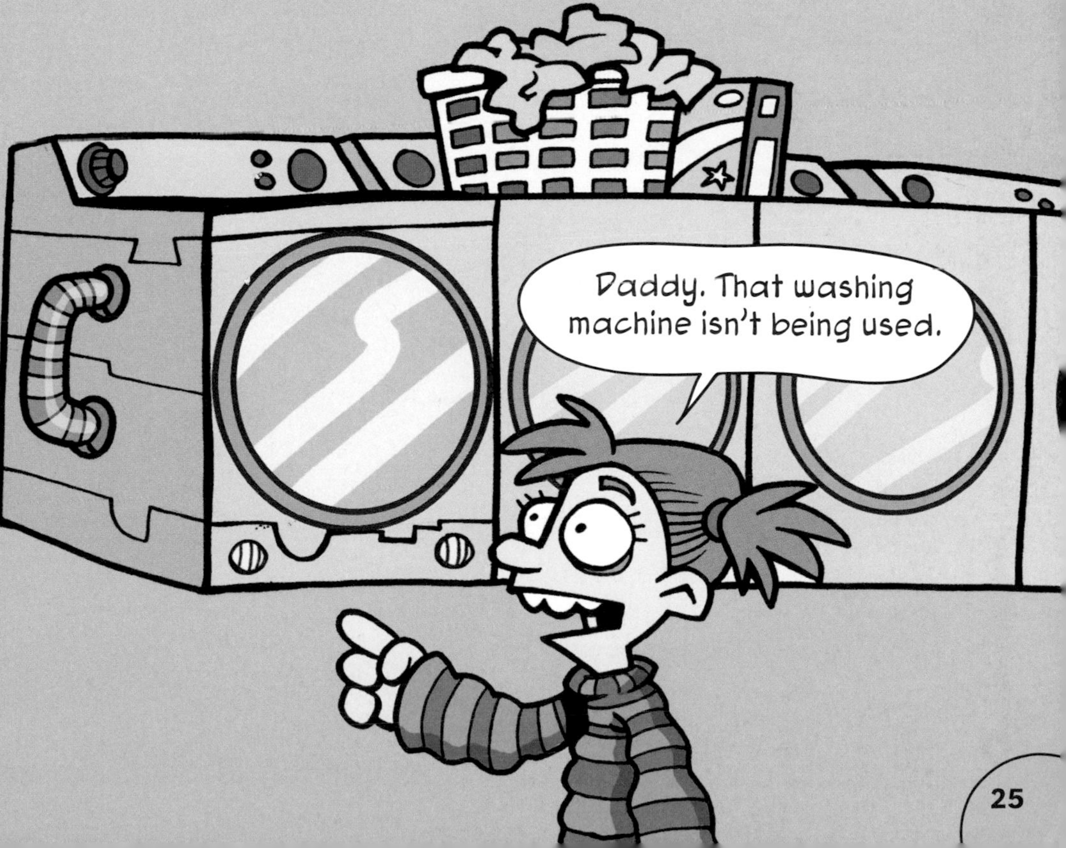
Daddy. That washing machine isn't being used.

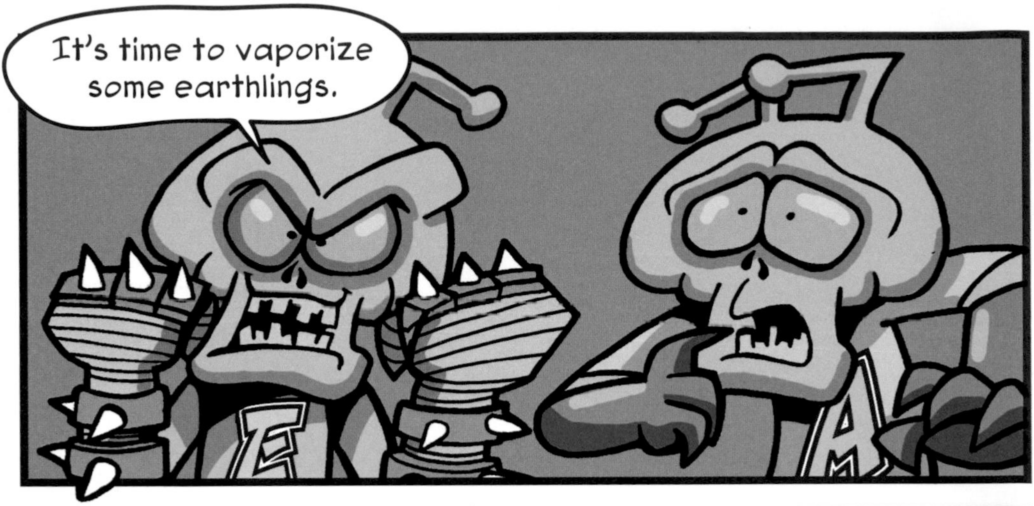
It's time to vaporize some earthlings.

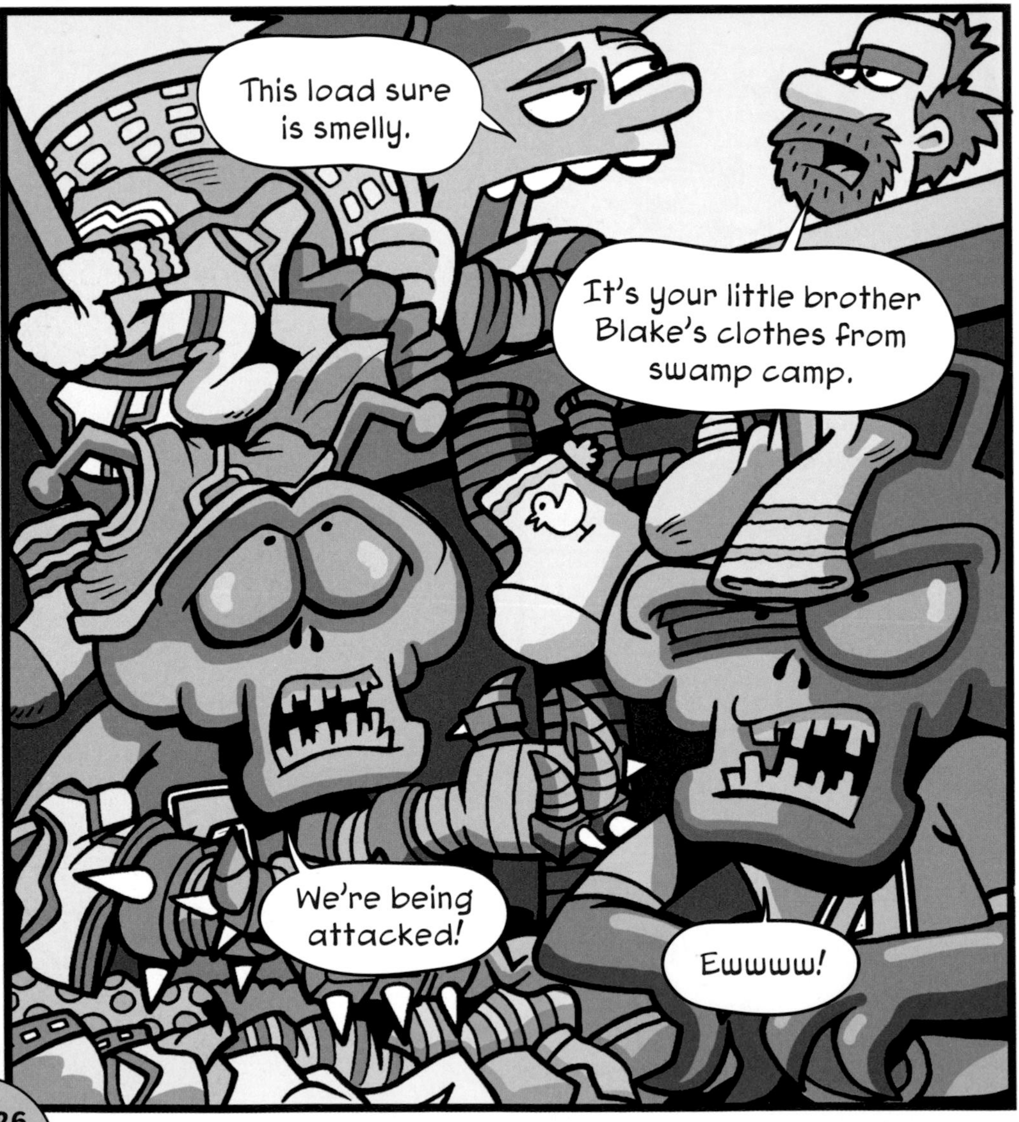
This load sure is smelly.
It's your little brother Blake's clothes from swamp camp.
We're being attacked!
Ewwww!

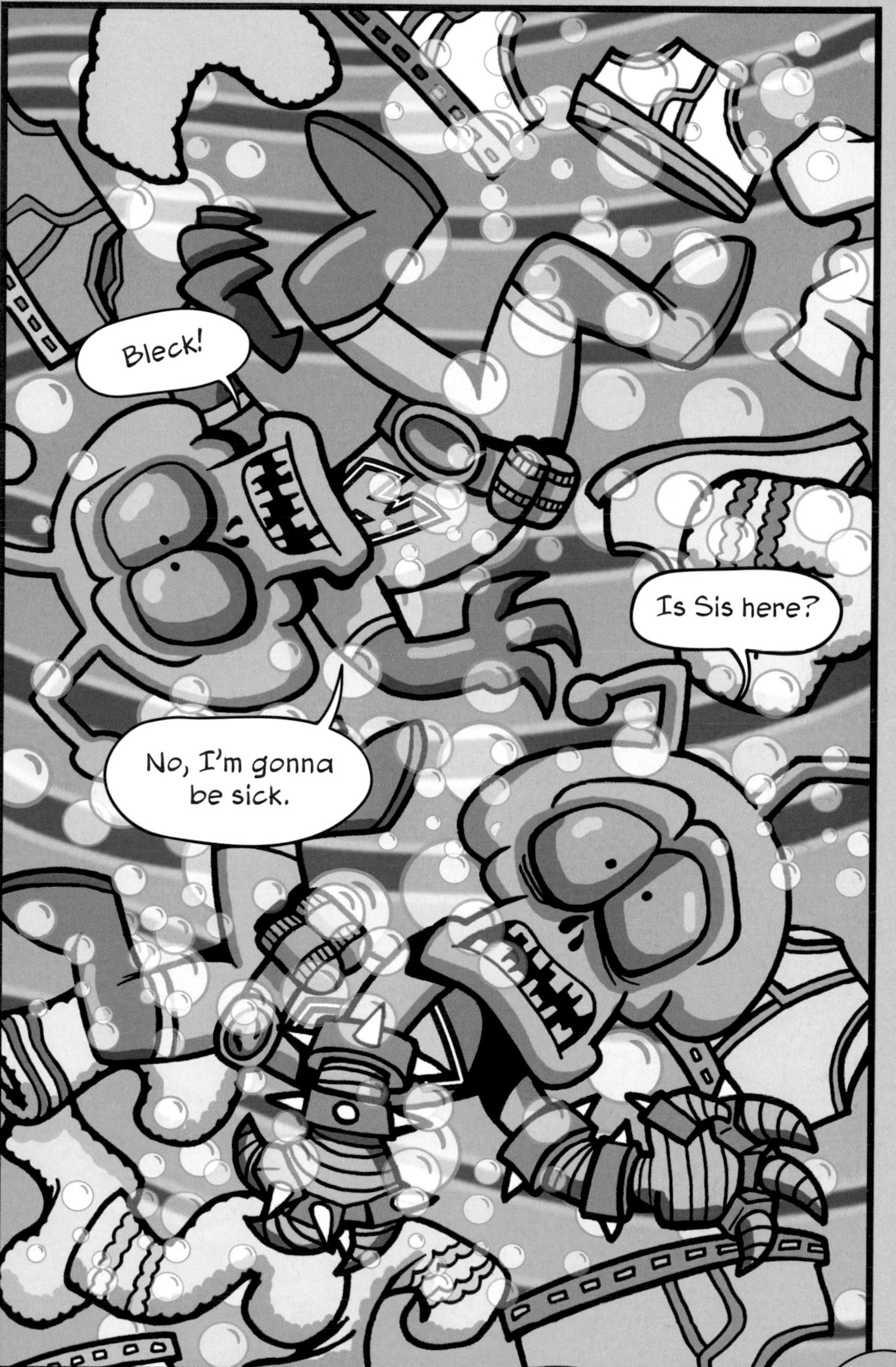
Bleck!
Is Sis here?
No, I'm gonna be sick.

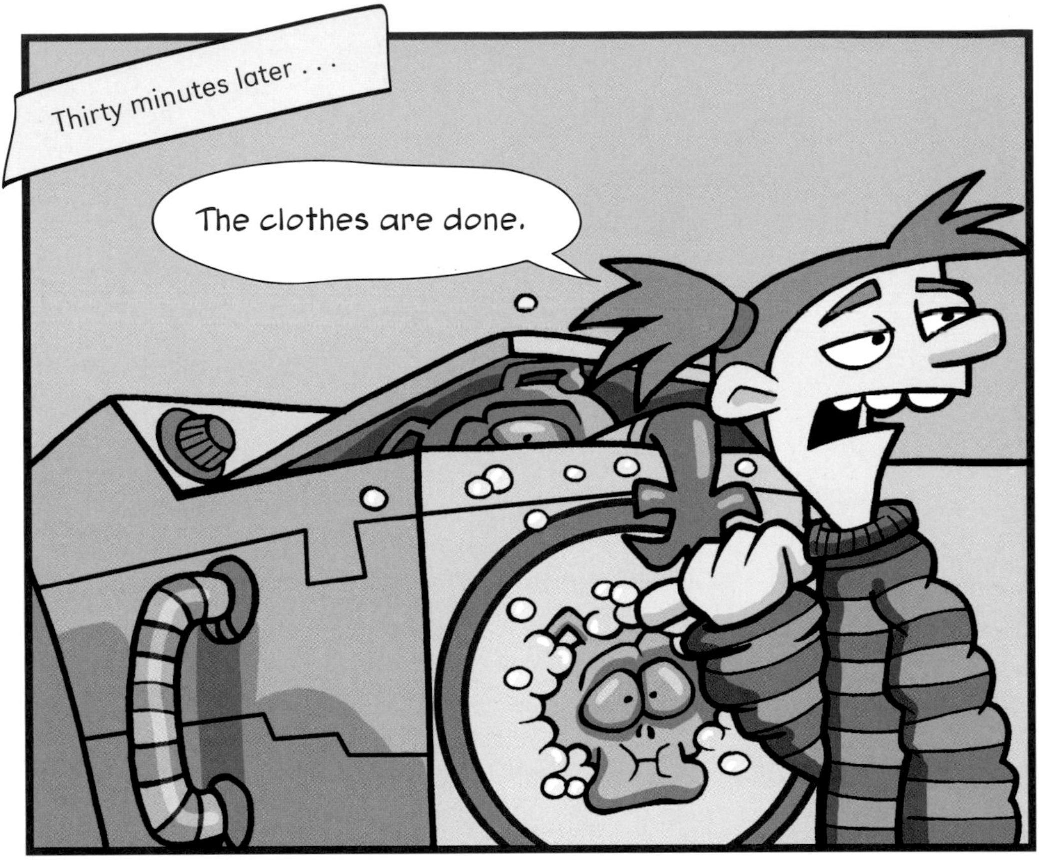
Thirty minutes later . . .
The clothes are done.

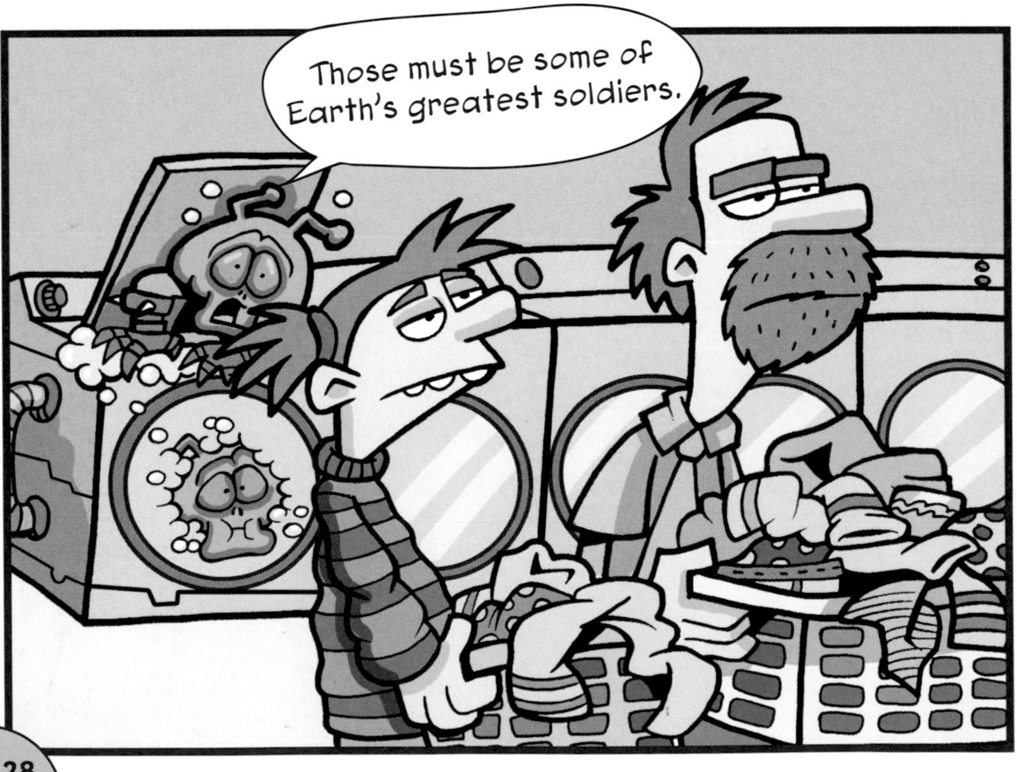
Those must be some of Earth's greatest soldiers.

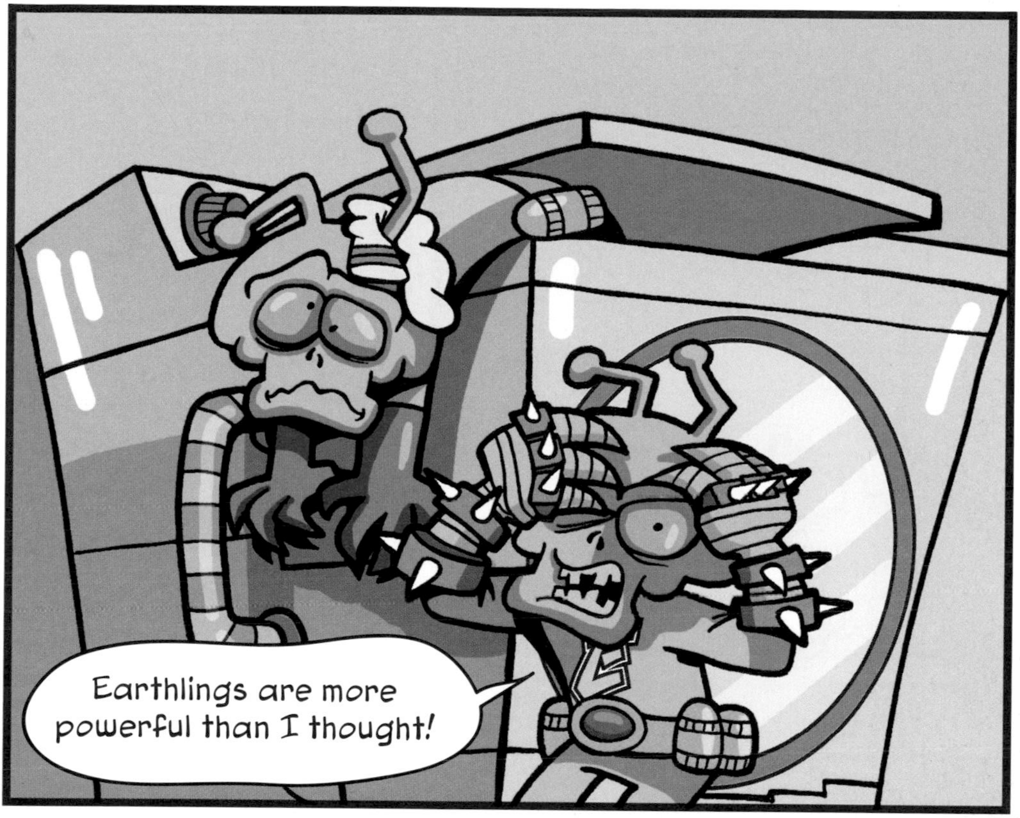
Earthlings are more powerful than I thought!

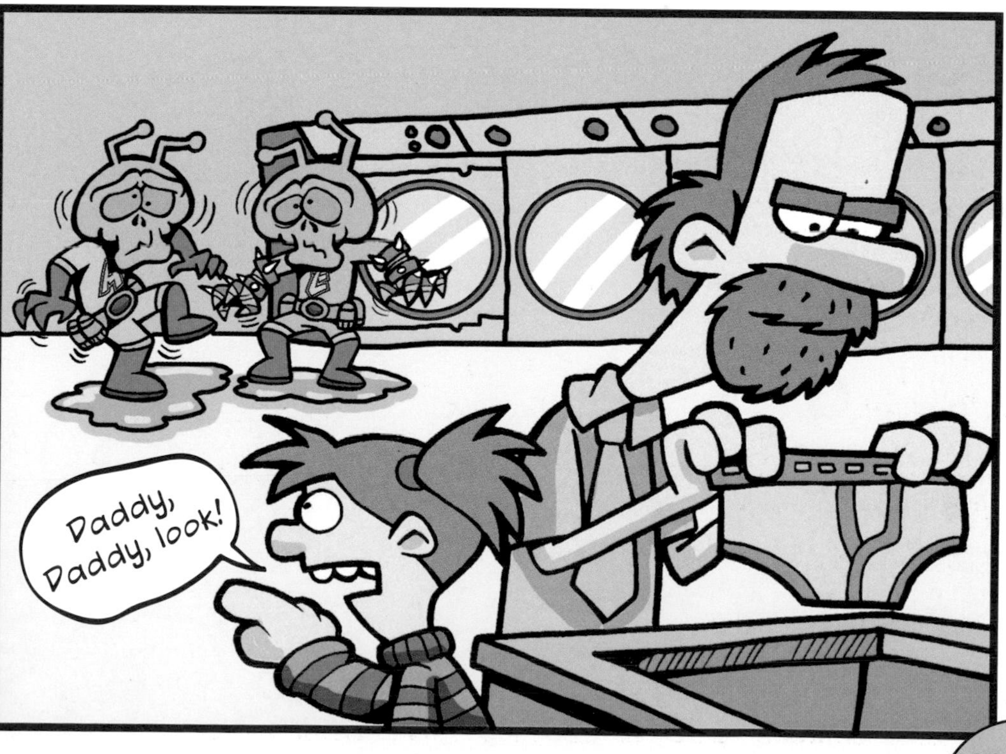
Daddy, Daddy, look!

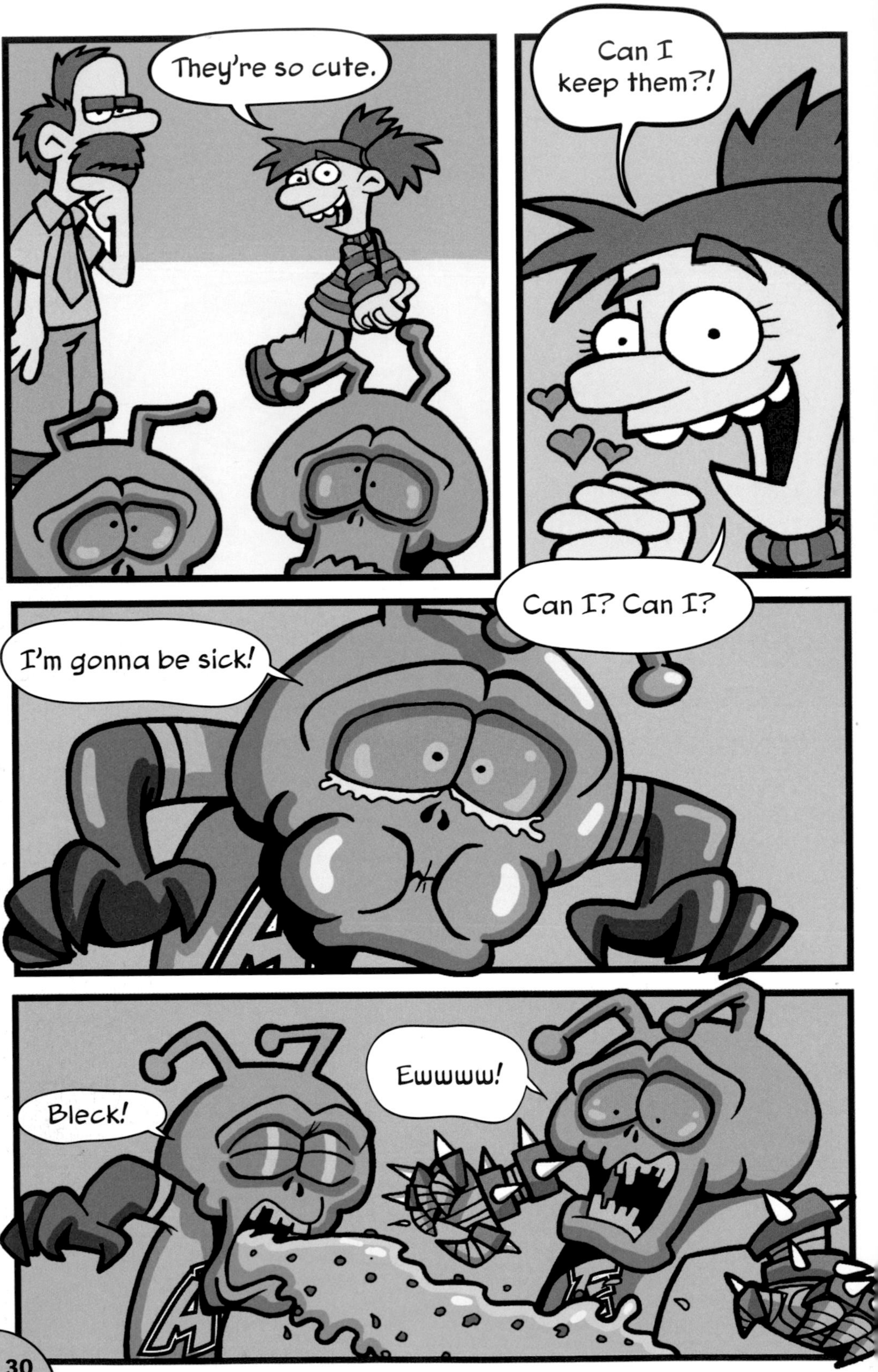
They're so cute.
Can I keep them?!
Can I? Can I?
I'm gonna be sick!
Bleck!
Ewwww!

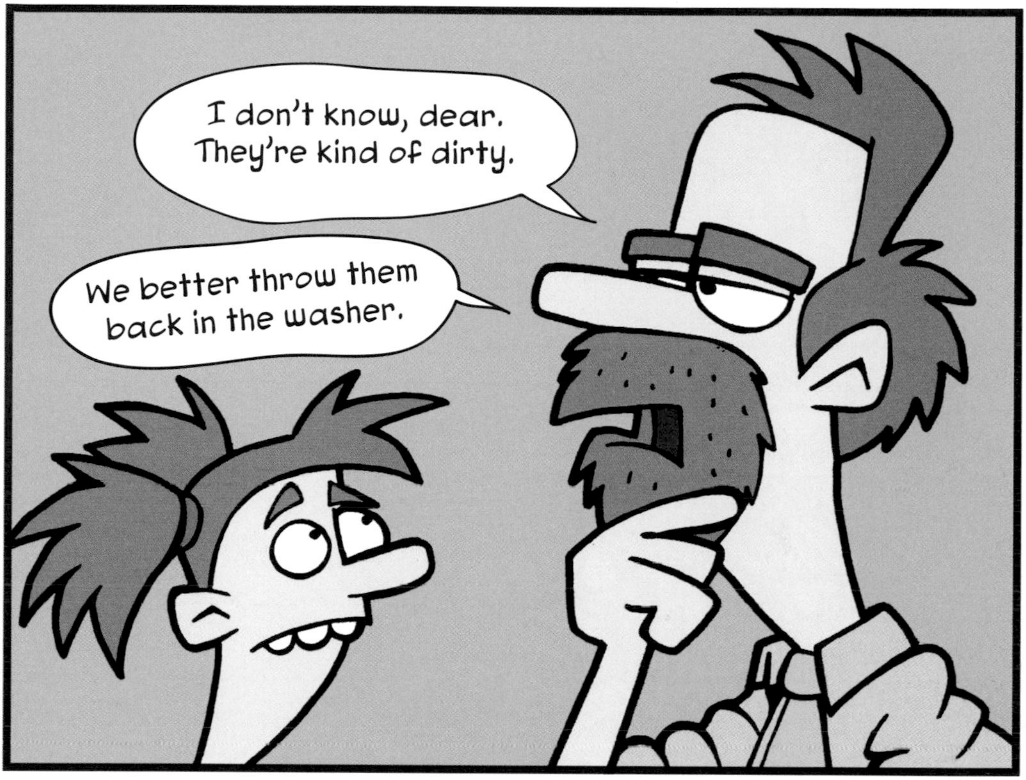
I don't know, dear.
They're kind of dirty.
We better throw them
back in the washer.

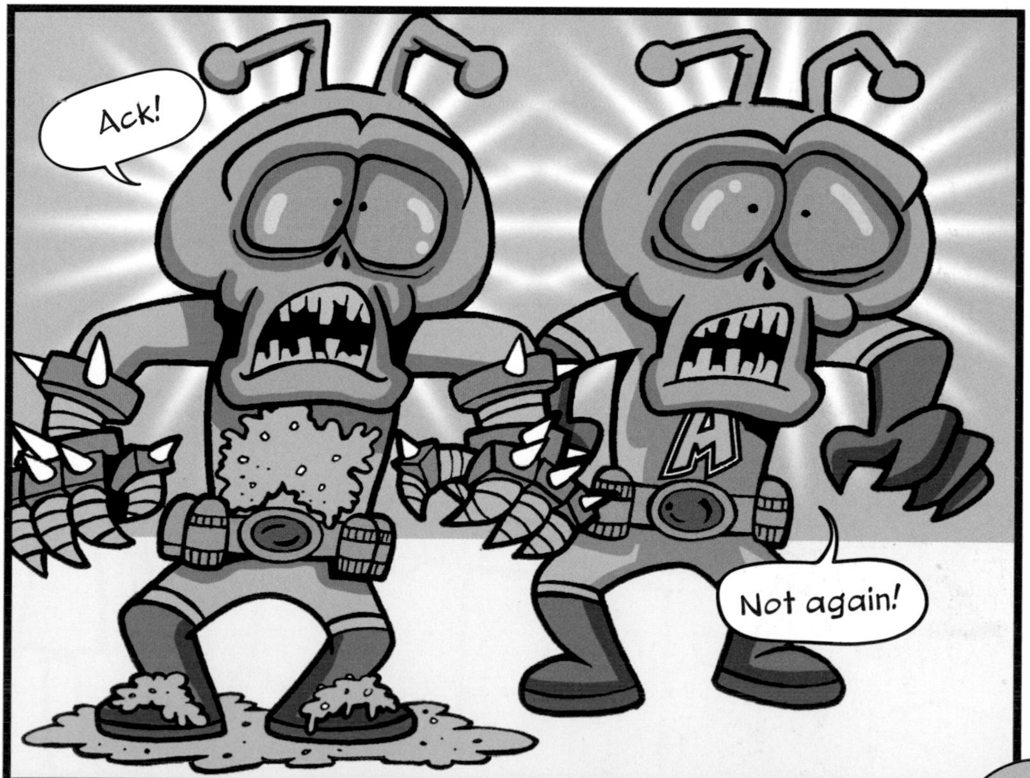
Ack!
Not again!

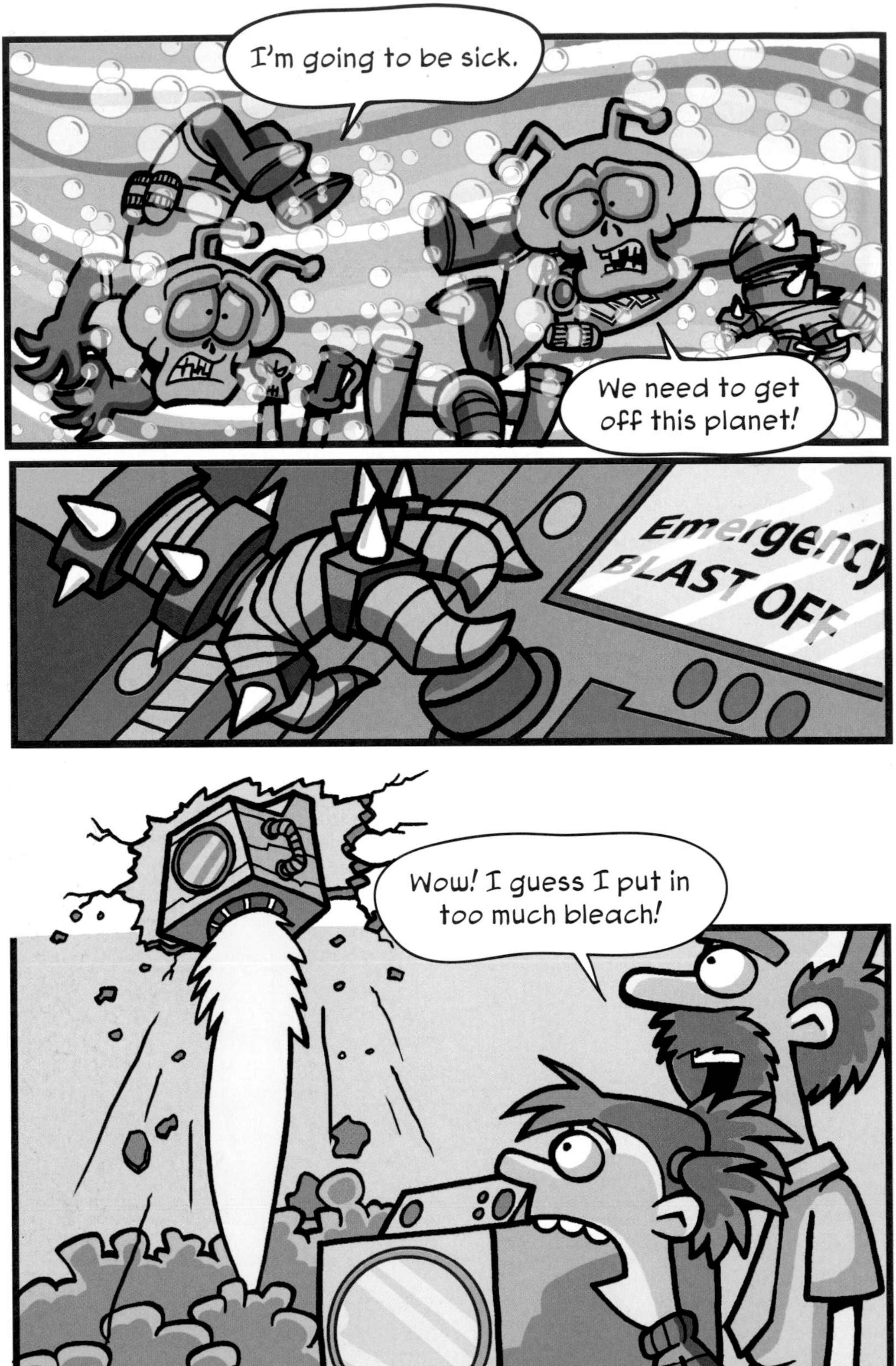
I'm going to be sick.
We need to get off this planet!
Emergency BLAST OFF
Wow! I guess I put in too much bleach!

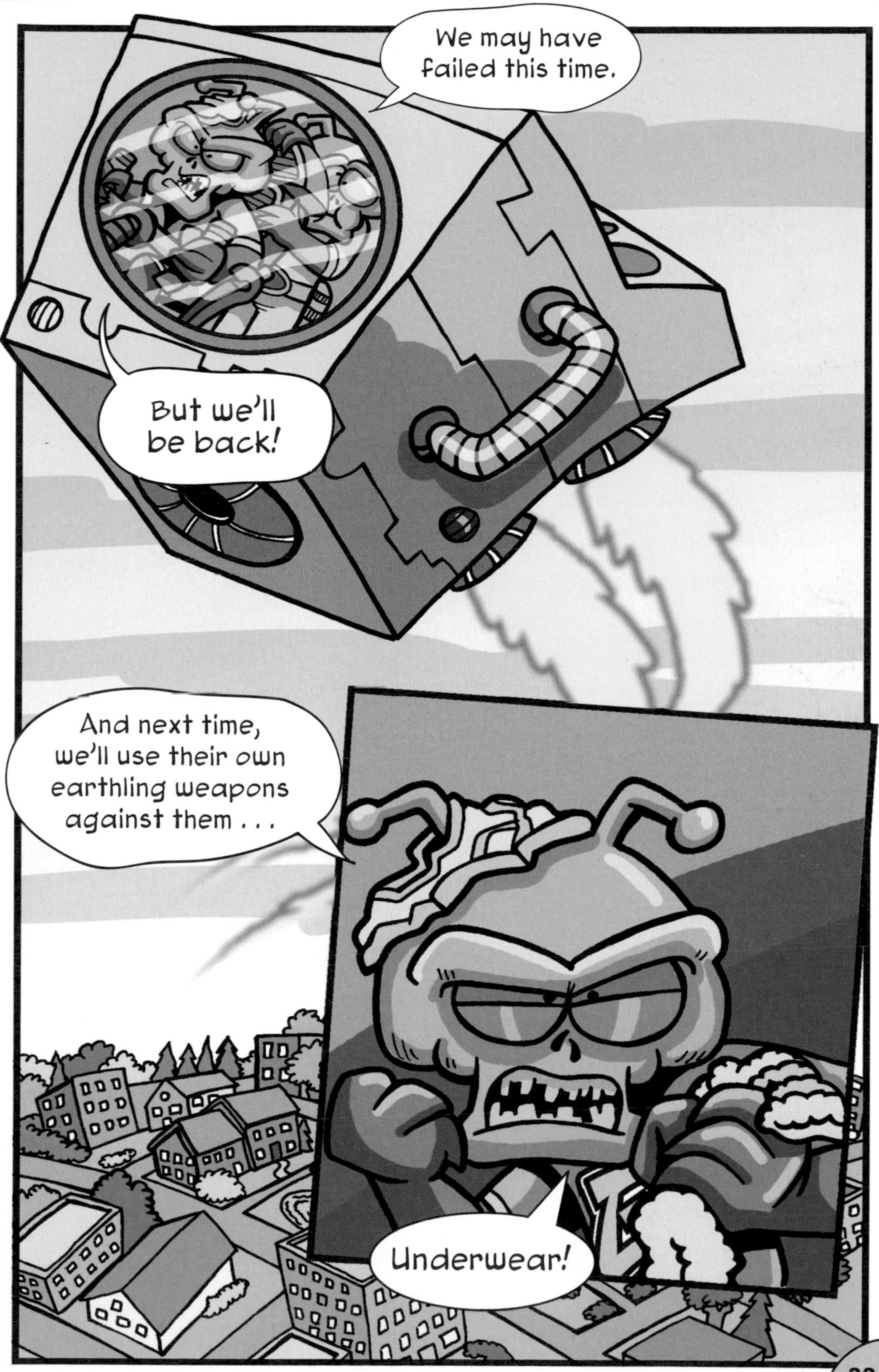
We may have failed this time.
But we'll be back!
And next time, we'll use their own earthling weapons against them . . .
Underwear!

ABOUT THE AUTHOR

Blake A. Hoena spends his nights holding a laundry basket of dirty clothes and staring up at the stars. He doesn't know if there really are aliens, but he wants to be ready just in case Eek and Ack return to Earth. This is the first book he's written about aliens. Usually he writes about dogs, pigs, sheep, and camels.

ABOUT THE ILLUSTRATOR

Steve Harpster has loved to draw funny cartoons, mean monsters, and goofy gadgets since he was able to pick up a pencil. In first grade, he was able to avoid his writing assignments by working on the pictures for stories instead. Steve was able to land a job drawing funny pictures for books, and that's really what he's best at. Steve lives in Columbus, Ohio, with his wonderful wife, Karen, and their sheepdog, Doodle.

GLOSSARY

conquest (KON-kwest)—to defeat and take control of something

hover (HUHV-ur)—to remain in one place while flying, which is the right way to use a rocket pack when playing indoors

kabobbler (ka-BOB-lur)—any tool used to fix a spaceship; a de-fizzler also works

Milky Way (MILK-ee WAY)—the galaxy that includes Earth, our entire solar system, and about 100 billion stars!

vaporize (VAY-pur-eyez)—to turn anything solid into smoke, mist or steam; usually done with a vaporizer, an alien's favorite invention

whizzler speed (WHIZ-lur speed)—faster than twizzler speed but slower than swizzler speed. Whizzler is the normal speed for a washing machine flying through space.

EEK AND ACK'S GALAXY OF FACTS

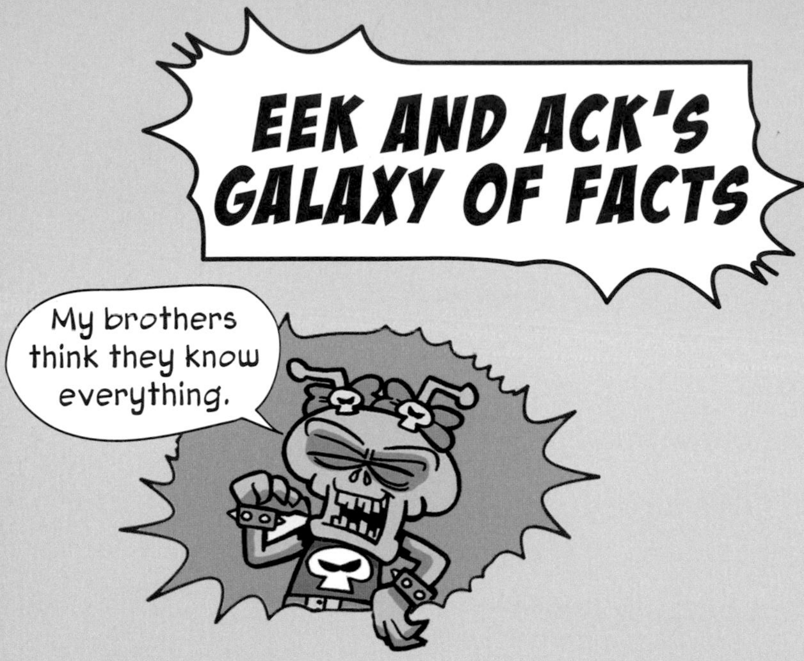
My brothers think they know everything.

Did you know that a blue moon isn't really blue? "Blue moon" is the name for the second full moon that shows up in a month. This only happens every two and a half to three years. That's why, when something rare happens, we say it happens "once in a blue moon."

Scientists know more about outer space than they do about our deepest oceans.

One day on the Pluto is the same amount of time as a week here on Earth. Wow, and you thought the school day lasted forever!

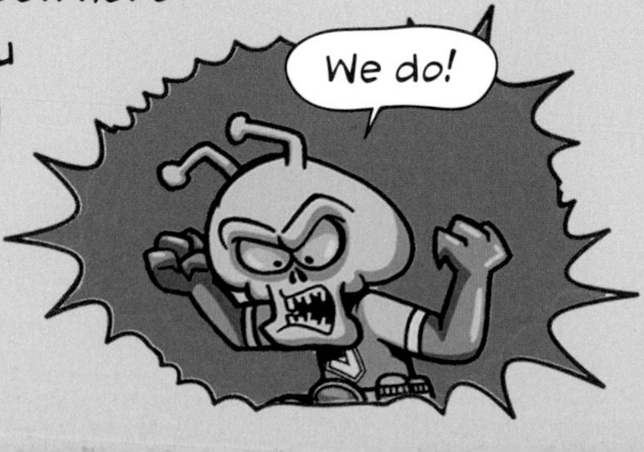
We do!

If you shouted in space, even someone standing right next to you couldn't hear you. Sound doesn't travel in space. Aliens have all the luck!

Think you want to count all the stars in the galaxy? If you counted one star each second, it would take you three thousand years. Hmm, should have started sooner!

If you were driving 75 miles per hour, it would take you about 258 days to circle one of Saturn's rings.

What foot did Neil Armstrong use to step onto the moon? His left.

DISCUSSION QUESTIONS

1. Eek and Ack have very different personalities. How do they react differently to situations in the story? Use an event in the story to explain your answer.

2. Eek is happy to be working on his spaceship, until his sister Bleck shows up. Why does Eek's attitude change around his older sister?

3. Eek and Ack's spaceship looks like a washing machine, and they crash land outside a laundromat. Do you think the author planned this from the start? How would the story be different if Eek and Ack landed somewhere else, for instance, such as an animal shelter or a bowling alley?

1. Hurry, hurry! A UFO has just landed in your backyard! Describe what the ship looks like, if the aliens are friendly, and why they have come to Earth. If it helps, draw a picture first.

2. Imagine you lived on a faraway planet. Describe how things would be different because of your alien home. What would school be like, what type of pets would you have, how would you play your favorite sports? Describe your life.

3. What if Eek and Ack succeeded in conquering Earth? What would things be like on our planet if two alien kids ran things? Write about it!

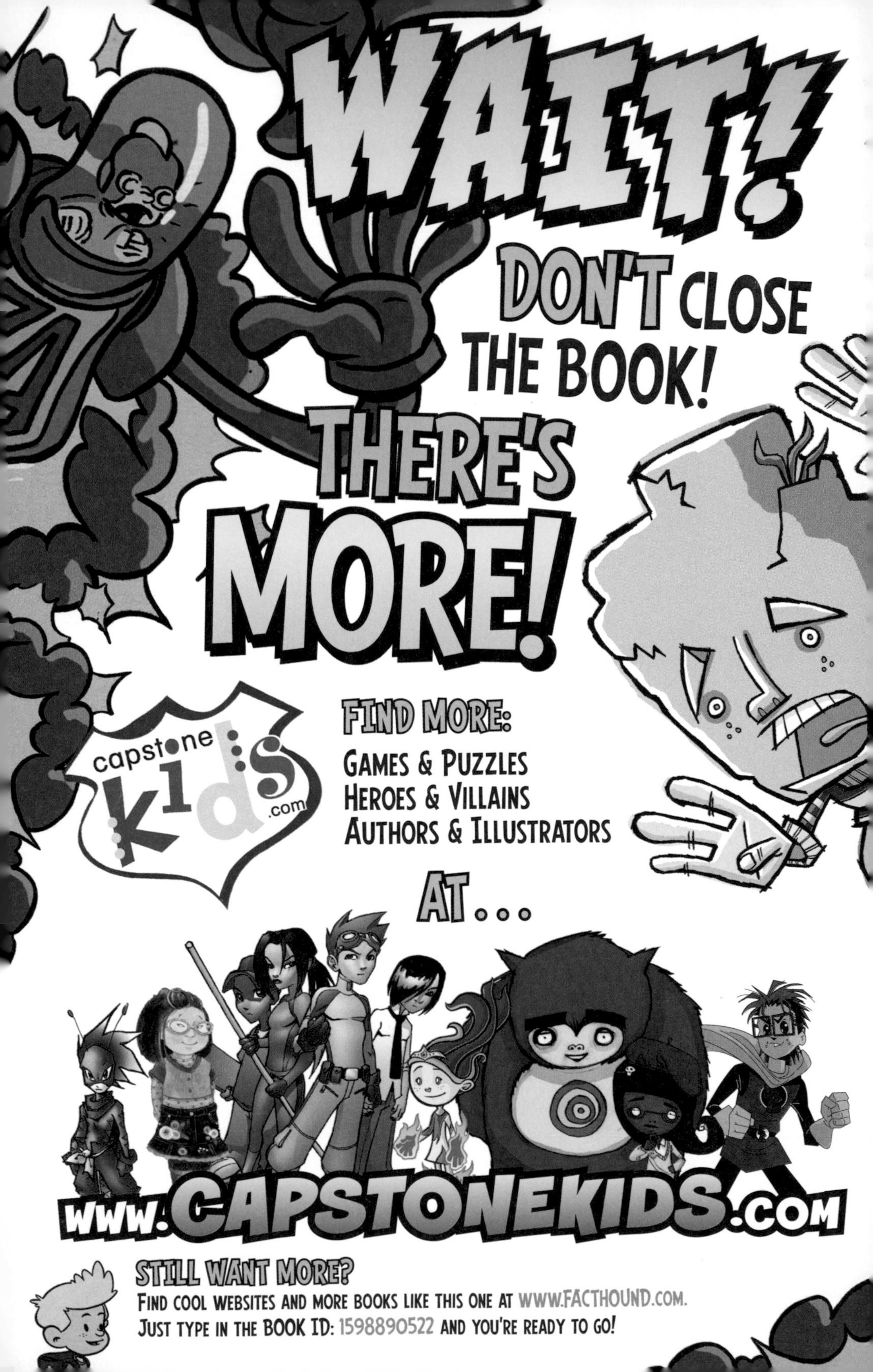
WAIT!
DON'T CLOSE THE BOOK!
THERE'S MORE!
capstone kids .com
FIND MORE:
GAMES & PUZZLES
HEROES & VILLAINS
AUTHORS & ILLUSTRATORS
AT...
WWW.CAPSTONEKIDS.COM
STILL WANT MORE?
FIND COOL WEBSITES AND MORE BOOKS LIKE THIS ONE AT WWW.FACTHOUND.COM.
JUST TYPE IN THE BOOK ID: 1598890522 AND YOU'RE READY TO GO!

GRAPHIC SPARKS

One boring afternoon, the terrible twosome of Eek and Ack come up with a sinister plot. They'll spend the day doing something deviously fun — conquering that weird, far-away planet, Earth!

"Bold and captivating."
— **School Library Journal**

MORE OUT OF THIS WORLD ADVENTURES!

EEK & ACK
The Puzzling Pluto Plot
by Blake A. Hoena
illustrated by Steve Harpster
STONE ARCH Science Fiction
EEK & ACK
Beyond the Black Hole
EEK & ACK
Ooze Slingers from Outer Space
by Blake A. Hoena
illustrated by Steve Harpster
STONE ARCH Science Fiction

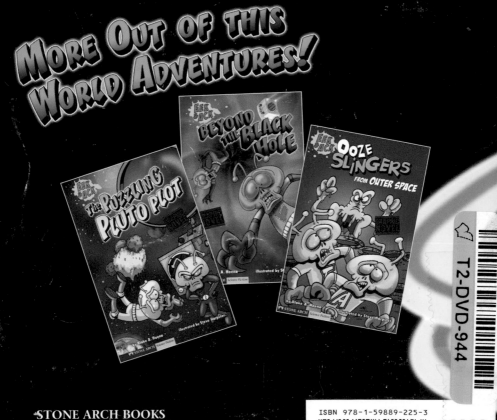

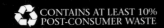

STONE ARCH BOOKS
Capstone Publishers • www.stonearchbooks.com
008-010 RL: 1.7 Guided Reading Level: H

CONTAINS AT LEAST 10% POST-CONSUMER WASTE

ISBN 978-1-59889-225-3
90000
9 781598 892253